HIS TEDDY BEAR

EVE LANGLAIS

Copyright © April 2011, Eve Langlais

2nd Edition Released April 2016

Cover art by © Razzle Dazzle Design March 2016

Produced in Canada

Published by Eve Langlais

http://www.EveLanglais.com

ALL RIGHTS RESERVED

His Teddy Bear is a work of fiction and the characters, events and dialogue found within the story are of the author's imagination and are not to be construed as real. Any resemblance to actual events or persons, either living or deceased, is completely coincidental.

No part of this book may be reproduced or shared in any form or by any means, electronic or mechanical, including but not limited to digital copying, file sharing, audio recording, email and printing without permission in writing from the author.

eBook ISBN: 978-1-988328-00-3

Ingram ISBN: 978-1-77384-015-4

CHAPTER 1

I need to get laid. The pulsating thought—make that carnal need—had brought him to the town's bar tonight of all nights. His cynical side wanted to snort at the expectancy imbuing the air inside the crowded tavern as folks from all around gathered for the yearly spectacle known as the Were-For-All. All across North America, shape-shifters of all castes were meeting up at designated bars and halls for a night of dancing, drinking, and, for a lucky few, finding their *one*. Reece's intention was much simpler—sweaty, hardcore sex. And not the vanilla type of fun that could be found with a human female. He craved some hard pounding, nails-raking-down-his-back sex, and only another shape-shifter could handle that need.

Not that he'd told his grandmother that tidbit.

How could he when her eyes lit up at his mention of his destination? She hadn't lost hope he'd find his mate, even though he'd reached the ripe old age of thirty-five. Truth be told, Reece kind of hoped he'd find her too—having a welcoming wife waiting in his bed after a hard day's work had its appeal—but having spent years watching his buddies fall in love —with sickening puppy-dog eyes and whipped attitudes—he both dreaded and ached for it.

But it looked as if this wouldn't be the year he found his *one*. None of the females in attendance grabbed his attention or made his wolf howl. Not that he really cared, or so he lied to himself, as he sat at the bar with some of his packmates, tossing back whiskey shots. His vantage point allowed him to look over and, in most cases, dismiss the females in attendance—*too young, too old, too chunky, way too ugly, married...* Reece could afford his picky attitude. At six-feet-three, muscled, and with a face more handsome than Brad Pitt's, according to the ladies, he ultimately decided who would grace his bed.

Reece had his eye on a shapely blonde he hadn't tasted before when the outside door opened and a scent wafted in that roused his slumbering beast. His wolf shook itself awake in his mind and, with a mental yip, demanded Reece explore the newcomers. Intrigued at his wolf's unusual behavior, Reece inhaled deeply, and a sweet aroma tickled his nose—

and stirred his cock—a delicious blend of Ivory soap, cherry lip-gloss, and *woman. My woman.* The realization almost blew him away, even as his prick hardened and his wolf growled in anticipation. So many years he'd waited and wondered, and now, at last, in walked the woman who'd not only take care of his sexual needs but also bear his pups.

Time to meet the lucky lady.

Reece took a deep breath, surprised at his nervousness—*It's just a woman*—and turned to meet the female he'd take as his own. *My mate.*

He spun around slowly on the barstool, ignoring the question from the packmate at his side. His eyes scanned the entrance to the bar, where a group of women stood, milling about and laughing. They appeared a mostly attractive bunch, tall and slender with hair in varying shades of the rainbow. But as he scanned their ranks, he spotted a shorter form with cropped hair bobbing among them. He frowned and directed his attention back to the model-type beauties, trying to pinpoint which of them was about to become the lucky recipient of his cock, but to his annoyance, his eyes kept returning to the barely visible squat one. *Don't tell me my mate is going to be some midget?* Given his stature, he'd always dated—and fucked—women with a bit of height. Surely fate, or whatever force guided mates together, wouldn't be so cruel as to pair him up with someone too tiny to accommodate?

Whatever Reece's thoughts on the matter, his wolf pulsed beneath his skin, its excitement making it fight for control. Reece tightened his leash on his inner beast and mentally commanded it to settle down. While the place was packed with shifters, it was considered bad form—not to mention juvenile—to lose control of one's beast in public, no matter the reason, or tasty scent.

Chastised, his wolf settled down with a whine. Reece slid off his stool to walk toward the gaggle of women.

"Hot damn, I think Reece is about to get collared."

Reece ignored the jibe of his pack brother behind him and the laughter of the others as they made fun of his predicament. He couldn't blame them for their humor, given his ribbing at their expense when they'd met their mates and turned into pussy-whipped puppies. Not that he'd allow that to happen to him. He had more self-control and pride than to allow a woman to lead him by the nose, mate or not.

He reached the outer edge of the group of women, and his wolf growled at the unmistakable aroma of bear. He lifted a brow in surprise. The only bear groups he knew of lived in the Rockies, and from his understanding, they ventured forth only rarely, preferring the company of their own kind.

The chattering subsided as he scanned each of the women's features, knowing even as he did that the one he sought hid behind the outer ring. As if commanded, the minor sea of females parted, revealing the short form of the woman with the glossy cap of hair that he'd seen from the crowd. His beast yipped in excitement, but Reece groaned in disbelief.

No fucking way. My mate's a chubby?

TEDDY DIDN'T WANT to go to the bar, even if the reason for the trip was for them to mix and mingle at the yearly Were-For-All. But she'd promised her mother she'd look after her younger sister who was in search of a mate with a single-mindedness Teddy didn't understand. *Why is it all the women I know are desperate to find a man?* Teddy sure as heck wasn't, even though she knew her mother prayed she'd settle down and pop out a few cubs.

Teddy, though, had no interest in marriage. The idea of letting a man dictate to her—and possibly hurt her—didn't appeal at all. Not to mention, she wasn't keen on becoming some cub-bearing machine. At the ripe age of thirty-two, she'd resigned herself to life as a spinster, not that she minded. She loved her job as a kindergarten teacher. She also owned her own home and possessed a black book at home with a list of names she could call when the need for battery-less fun struck her. Although that list had dwindled down in recent years as the men she knew kept meeting and settling down with their mates.

Filling up her black book with new names was one of the reasons she'd allowed herself to be persuaded to come on this trip. A few hours away from home, this town in the Northwest Territories provided the perfect fodder to expand her sexual choices in partners.

The moment she walked into the bar, her nose twitched and she took a step backwards. Her sister—a blonde Amazon who looked nothing like her—looked down with a frown.

"What's wrong, Teddy?"

"I smell something—" She bit off the word *good* before it left her lips but couldn't help thinking it as she inhaled deeply. A yummy, distinctly male scent set her girly parts tingling, and her eyes widened in surprise.

It can't be. Teddy wanted to deny her senses, but she'd heard her four already mated sisters gush enough about the experience to know what she felt. *My mate is in this bar.*

Trepidation, anticipation, and excitement tried to clutch her and make her a prisoner of her hormones, but Teddy shrugged them off. She wasn't some naïve little girl who would swoon at the feet of the man fate had chosen for her. But she couldn't prevent curiosity from bubbling forth, and she craned on tiptoe to see if she could spot the man that biology—and an inexplicable force that liked to meddle in shape-shifters' lives—deemed her perfect mate. Her plan to check him out first ended up foiled, though, surrounded as she was by her sister and cousins, all of whom towered over her by six inches or more.

She frowned as she fought an urge to push through the ranks of bodies to see him. She refused to act too eager. She had too much self-respect to act like a desperate sow in heat.

Apparently, he didn't share the same trepidation because if the sizzle along her nerve endings was any indicator, he approached. Her bear, usually dormant this cold time of the year, stretched in her mind and chuffed. Teddy's mouth went dry and although her mind screamed, "Run," her feet stayed rooted to the floor.

The wall of bodies in front of her parted, and Teddy found herself staring at a man's stomach covered in a plaid shirt. Her eyes flicked down to check out his package first—*Screw propriety. I want a man with heavy equipment.* Pleased at the bulge she saw, her gaze traveled up the length of him from his tapered waist to his broad chest and wide shoulders. The man was immense, and she idly wondered if having sex with him would require mountain climbing skills.

She thought she heard him make a noise through the roaring in her ears, but as she inhaled his scent, now close enough for her to savor his unique flavor, she grimaced. *A wolf?* In the off chance she did eventually meet her one, Teddy had really hoped for a bear like herself.

Apparently, she wasn't the only one disappointed because when her eyes finally met the deep brown ones of the man her bear insisted was their mate, she could see shock and distaste reflected in his eyes.

I guess he doesn't like short women with curves. Teddy didn't allow for one moment his evident distaste for her shape to bring her down. It had taken her years to overcome her personal issues with her body size—although some of her more painful moments stubbornly lingered to taunt her and shrivel her confidence at inopportune moments. She'd finally reached a point in her life where she now loved her lush body—most of the time—and so did the men who shared her bed. And if the giant wolf didn't like it? Too bad. She wasn't that interested in acquiring a mate in the first place, no matter what her agitated bear thought.

His brow creased, and he opened his mouth as if to speak, but Teddy didn't wait to hear what he had to say, not when his eyes and body language had already said it all.

Teddy snorted, making her disdain for him evident, and pushed past him in the direction of the bar. The electric sizzle that jolted her as her body brushed his in passing caught her off guard and, judging by his sucked-in breath, took him by surprise, too. But the liquid heat pooling in her pussy and the tightening of her nipples didn't stop her from making a beeline to the bar.

The stools were all occupied, but she squeezed herself in between a pair and waved at the frazzled barkeep. She ordered a tequila shot and downed it straight. The heat from the alcohol spread but didn't come close to making the molten arousal from her brief contact with the goliath disappear. She ordered another two shots.

Her youngest sister, Georgie, slipped in beside her at the bar and arched a brow. "What the heck happened back there?"

"I met my mate," Teddy answered nonchalantly before downing a second shot of burning fire.

Georgie's face knitted into a frown as she looked from Teddy to a spot behind her, where Teddy assumed the behemoth stood. "I don't get it. Shouldn't you guys be, like, all over each other? I mean, I thought when you met your mate it was like some uncontrollable urge."

"Oh, my bear wants him all right, but I'm not interested." Teddy lied to her sister. Truthfully, she fought not only her beast but also her libido, which kept yammering at her to go back and maul the jerk. *No way.* Teddy tossed back the third tequila.

Georgie's mouth rounded into an 'O' of surprise, and Teddy could see the questions brimming in her eyes. Not in the mood to answer them—even as she knew her sister would probably go slug the jerk in question for making her feel ugly—Teddy moved away from the bar and zigzagged her way to the jammed dance floor. Surrounded by gyrating, sweaty bodies, she let the music envelope her and clear her mind, the hard bass a steady tempo for her to undulate and shake to.

It didn't take long for a male body to start moving in time to hers, but to her annoyance, she couldn't focus on her dance partner. Instead, all her senses were tuned to *his* presence. Like a dark shadow at her back, she felt his eyes boring a hole through her, his ire palpable. When her partner grabbed her hands and whirled her, she had her eyes open, and thus, she caught a glimpse of the wolf's face—grim and foreboding.

She stuck her tongue out at him and then laughed as his countenance darkened even further.

She twirled back to face her dance partner with a smug smile on her face. *Go bother someone else, Mr. Wolf, because this Little Red Riding Hood isn't about to let you taste her goodies.*

His growing irritation went a long way toward soothing her bruised ego because, while she could protest all she wanted that she liked herself and her body just fine, a teensy-tiny part of her ached that her mate, found after all these years, didn't find her attractive.

His loss.

She pushed him from her mind and inwardly growled at her bear to shut up about it. Mating urge or not, she wouldn't get with a man who found her unattractive. Decided, she put all her focus on the guy in front of her, who had no problem with her curves. Teddy inched closer to him, letting her body brush his in a more intimate dance. *I don't need a mate to have some sweaty fun.*

CHAPTER 2

*R*eece couldn't believe the short, chubby woman looking up at him was his mate. Didn't fate know he liked his women tall and slim?

Even more astonishing was the dismissal in her vivid blue eyes when their gazes met. Before he could say a word, she snorted with clear disdain and pushed past him.

With that simple touch, lightning struck. Reece sucked in a breath as the brief contact set his body aflame—and instantly hardened his cock. Strange though, extra curves didn't usually give him the urge to bend a girl over and take her. But it seemed his usual preferences didn't apply at the moment because he couldn't deny an overwhelming need to have her.

A need that appeared one-sided.

As if she cared not a whit and hadn't sensed a thing, she sauntered away from him to the bar and signaled the bartender. Reece knew he must look a sight, gaping after her like an idiot. But seriously, while he saw no problem with his aversion of her general shape, he found himself stunned at her evident dislike of him. *Women love me!*

He couldn't stop staring at her as he waited for her to turn and face him. How could she not when everything in his being screamed at him to claim her? *Surely she feels the same pull?* But ignore him she did as she tossed back a few shots and murmured with a tall blonde who'd arrived to join her.

When the little bear did finally leave the bar, it wasn't to come back to him. Oh no. Instead, she moved farther away as she shimmied her way onto the packed dance floor.

Reece couldn't stop his feet from moving in her direction while his eyes tracked her. Self-respect screamed that he treat her indifferently—tit for tat—but his wolf and rod had different thoughts on the matter. His cock refused to play dead and, to his disbelief, thickened ever further as he watched her short and curvy frame gyrate on the dance floor. Her rounded bottom jiggled in a way his cock found much too fascinating, and his jeans became tight and confining.

Reece dropped his hands to his crotch to cover

his evident arousal, not that anyone paid him any attention—not even the woman his agitated wolf howled was their mate.

Then a feeling he'd never experienced before, but had seen all too often in his mated friends, engulfed him. Jealousy. He wanted to fight it, but it wasn't just his wolf who freaked when it noticed another shifter sidle up to her and start dancing. Reece couldn't prevent the growl that slipped past his lips when the other man touched *his woman* and swung her around.

And then the little witch had the nerve to stick her tongue out at him—a pink temptation that made him curl his hands into fists. Her laughter at his expense—a challenging and taunting sound—rung clear as a bell in his ears.

Reece knew he should walk away. She'd made it obvious she had no interest in him, and truly, she wasn't his type—even as his engorged cock made a lie of that assumption—but instead of returning to the bar to get rip-roaring drunk, he found himself a heartbeat later on the dance floor, prying the groping hands of the soon-to-be dead man from *his woman*.

The lycan who'd dared encroach on his territory took one look at Reece's snarling face and blanched. "She's all yours, man. I didn't know she was taken."

Reece could only growl as the man, who'd dared

touch her, slunk away. He longed to chase after him and inflict damage, but that would mean leaving his fated mate alone to start more mischief.

He turned his attention to the woman who'd managed to shoot his control to hell and disorder his life in less than thirty minutes flat. She returned his glare with a cool one of her own. She crossed her arms under plush breasts that strained over the edge of her top, and Reece's eyes became riveted by her shadowy cleavage. *Now that's what I call a pair of tits.*

He moved closer to her and noted the slight tremble in her frame—and smelled the desire her attitude tried to deny. He flicked his gaze back to her face and saw her blue eyes widen as he invaded her space. This close to her, Reece could no longer think coherently. All he knew was he had to touch her, claim her, *now*.

She fled before he could lay a hand on her and make her his.

Reece almost bellowed in frustration—his wolf didn't hold back and bayed loudly in his mind. Reece scrubbed a hand through his shaggy hair and blew out a frustrated breath. He refused to chase her like some lovesick swain—*I will not dance to her fucking tune.* His wolf had other ideas, though. It forced him to follow her. And Reece, his control already shredded, could do nothing to stop it.

His height allowed him to see her scooting, pushing, and squeezing her way through the bodies that seemed to have multiplied in the last few minutes. He had to move more slowly, his greater size forcing him to take care so as not to annoy the shifters in attendance. It wouldn't do to start a war because he accidentally shoved the wrong person. But the delay made him chafe.

He'd made it only halfway across the bar when the outside door opened and out she slipped, taking her driving-him-wild scent with her.

Unfortunately, though, her departure didn't take any of his feelings or urges with her. *Screw her. I am not going after her, mate or not.* He turned from the door and began to head toward the bar and the alcohol he suddenly desperately needed. He never reached it. Anxiety gripped him in tight tendrils, and his wolf pushed harder and harder, trying to take control.

Danger. His wolf's message came through loud and clear.

No longer caring if he started a war with every clan in the place, Reece shoved those in his path aside and stalked toward the outside door.

My mate needs me, whether she wants me or not.

&

TEDDY FLED the bar and the man inside driving her

nuts. She didn't have a choice because, had she stayed, she would have embarrassed herself by plastering herself to him and demanding he take her —*rough and wild*. It seemed the more she denied the mating call, the stronger it became.

Once outside, she wandered with no clear destination, knowing only that she needed to get away from the lights and noise—*him*. She dragged in heavy lungfuls of fresh, crisp spring air, but it didn't stop her racing heart or cool down her aching, hot pussy. Her bear showed her displeasure too, grumbling inside her mind, not understanding why they were standing outside, alone, when male temptation —and sinful sexual satisfaction—remained inside.

Teddy ignored her beast and let her feet take her farther away toward the beckoning comfort of the forest in the distance. She couldn't go back to the motel yet, not with her sister still inside having fun. But neither could she return to the bar. With nowhere to go, she kept walking.

She didn't immediately panic when her skin prickled at the presence of another shifter, although she mentally called herself all kinds of names for venturing so far from civilization by herself. *I know better than to put myself at risk with so many drunk and horny shifters nearby.* A quick sniff disabused her of the notion that her mate had come after her.

A form stepped from the shadows of the woods

in front of her, his steps weaving in a dance that alcoholics performed all too well. Teddy took a step back and whirled, planning to run back the way she'd come, an escape foiled by two more shapes approaching her from behind. *The bastards, they kept themselves downwind.* She couldn't stop the frisson of fear that shivered up her spine as she found herself surrounded by the drunken men. Even worse, all three were shape-shifters, which meant her more-than-human strength would be laughable against them if they meant her harm.

But perhaps she was overreacting. Just because they seemed intent on encroaching on her personal space didn't mean they had nefarious intent.

"What luck. A pretty little lady for us to share," one of them said with a leer, disabusing her quickly of that notion.

Teddy cursed her stupidity in wandering off alone. Her purpose on this trip was to protect her sister from this kind of scenario. Instead, she found herself caught. *Surely they aren't stupid enough to try anything with a bar full of shifters nearby?*

But the wild light in their eyes and tightening circle said otherwise.

"Listen, I wouldn't do this if I were you," she said a tad more breathlessly than she liked.

Loud guffaws met her feeble attempt at reasoning.

Teddy frowned and planted her hands on her hips, irritation taking the place of trepidation. "What are you, thickheaded? My mate's inside and sure to come after me any moment. So, run along before I tell him to eat your drunken asses." Teddy didn't for a moment believe her fabricated lie. After all, she'd made it pretty clear she had no interest in the man destined as her mate, but the idiots surrounding her didn't know that.

Unfortunately, her lie didn't even make them pause because the trio of men moved in closer. *I need to get out of here now.* Bravery was all well and good, but she lacked the size to back it up. It briefly occurred to her to call her bear, but the time it would take her to shift would leave her vulnerable. And, besides, her little brown bear against three werefoxes…

She decided speed and surprise would serve her better. Without any further hesitation, she ran at the stranger standing between her and the bar, but the guy behind her ended up faster. He snagged her with an arm around the waist and lifted her, even as she kicked and cursed.

"Put me down," she screeched, pissed that, once again, her smaller stature had left her vulnerable to the bigger bullies. They just laughed.

Hot tears of shame burned her eyes as the other

two men took advantage of her trapped position and groped her breasts.

I guess this is fate's punishment for turning down the mate she chose for me. Teddy couldn't help uttering a cry of pain as one of her assailants pinched her nipple hard.

Her cry didn't go unanswered.

A vicious howl shattered the night sky, and new tears flooded her eyes, this time of relief. She even tremulously smiled as the sudden scent of fear from her attackers filled the air. Elation filled her when her mate, a look of pure rage on his rugged face, came rushing in with swinging fists.

What do you know? The jerk came to my rescue.

CHAPTER 3

Reece emerged from the bar and sniffed the air, the distinctive scent of his mate sending him jogging off into the darkness. His wolf still paced in agitation, whining in his mind about danger. Reece ran faster, his enhanced eyesight adjusting to the evening gloom.

And when his ears caught her cry of pain—*How dare someone hurt my woman!*—he let forth a howl, an unearthly sound filled with rage.

Unthinking and uncaring of his own safety, he charged the group holding his struggling mate, his fists swinging as soon as he got within reach. Their paltry number—three against his one—weren't good odds for them, and even when they lay on the ground groaning, he remained dissatisfied. He wanted to pick them up and beat them again. Reece didn't hold back from booting one of them when the one who'd held his woman attempted to stand.

"Thanks for helping me out." Her soft words broke through his wall of seething anger.

He pivoted to face her, only to find her walking away from him—again. He ignored the thugs crawling off in the darkness to follow the minx who kept thwarting him.

Jaw clenched, he strode after her and grabbed her by the arm. She whirled to confront him, her eyes wide, but instead of fear on her face, he saw irritation.

"Let me go."

"You're my mate." He spat the words out through clenched teeth as he fought an urge to shake her.

She rolled her eyes. "Yeah, so my bear tells me. Personally, I think she's mistaken."

Reece didn't know whether to laugh at her provocative statement or be annoyed. He'd shared the same thought, but he found hearing her voice made him want to refute it. "The mating bond is never wrong."

"There's always a first time," she replied in a scoffing tone. "Besides, I saw the look on your face when you first saw me. You weren't happy. Don't even try and deny it."

"Fine then, I won't. You're chubby," he stated flatly. "And not my usual type." He blamed the adrenaline rushing through him and her continued rejection for his blunt words. Although, now that the initial shock of meeting her had worn off, despite her extra pounds, he found himself liking certain things about her, such as the way her generous bosom heaved as she took in a deep breath to reply.

"And you're a boorish dog who was obviously never housebroken," she replied caustically.

Despite himself, Reece admired her spunk. It was rare he came across a woman who didn't fear speaking her mind to him, annoying as her words might be. "So, what are we going to do about it?"

"Nothing." She pulled herself from his grasp and resumed walking away from him.

Like bloody hell. Before he knew what he planned, he'd grabbed her again. He placed his big hands on her waist and, in one fluid movement, both turned and lifted her until her lips were a hairsbreadth away. She stared at him with wide eyes, and her lips parted on a gasp. And even more astonishing, the sweet aroma of her arousal surrounded him.

"What do you think you're doing?" she demanded in a breathy voice.

He didn't answer. How could he when he wasn't even sure what he meant to do? Actually, that was a lie. He knew what he wanted, even as he didn't understand it.

He tasted her, his mouth claiming what was his,

and with that one fiery touch, his whole world tilted on its axis.

She held herself stiffly in his grasp at first, but as his lips slanted over hers, teasing and nibbling, she slowly relaxed and the scent of her desire grew thicker. When her arms came around his neck, Reece groaned, a sound she swallowed as she opened her mouth for him, allowing his tongue entry. He didn't waste the opportunity. He slipped his tongue into the warm recess of her mouth, her sweet taste and tantalizing scent driving him well beyond reason.

Instinct drove him, pushed him to claim her, mark her, *now*.

Holding her in midair as he did, he couldn't let his hands rove her body like he craved. And he feared letting her go lest she attempt to escape him again. He sank down, the coldness of the ground through his jeans not enough to douse the roaring inferno racing through his body. She straddled him, her hands clutching the fabric at his shoulders as she aggressively took over the kiss, her own misgivings apparently forgotten amidst the need to mate, which consumed them both. Her cleft, even with the layers between them, pressed against his groin, and he couldn't miss the heat that radiated from it.

His hands left the indent of her waist to slide

down and cup her ass. He squeezed her full cheeks, grunting as he discovered he actually enjoyed the ampleness of them. Her gasp of pleasure at his massage was just an added bonus. She pressed herself tighter to him, the voluptuousness of her bosom squashing against his chest, and he suddenly burned with a need to touch it. He pulled her shirt from the waistband of her pants and slid his hands up under the fabric. Her skin, smooth as silk, trembled at his callused touch. His seeking hands encountered the barrier of her bra, but with deft fingers, he unsnapped the impediment. She broke their kiss as she leaned back in invitation, and he cupped her heavy breasts, loving their weighty feel in his palms. And when he brushed a thumb over her nipple, it instantly blossomed into a tight bud. A quiver rocked her body, and he almost came at her erotic response to his touch.

He tugged her shirt up higher, needing to taste her pebbled berries. She arched back to accommodate him, and he took what she offered, his mouth latching onto one protruding nipple while his fingers toyed with the other. Her cries of pleasure surrounded him, urged him on, and he lost himself in the plumpness of her breasts.

Beautiful and bountiful. Never before had he feasted on breasts so full and natural. He buried his face in their softness and couldn't help wondering what it would feel like to slide his cock between them.

But that would have to wait for another time and place because his turgid cock demanded satiation. He drew her back in for a kiss, even as his hands found the button and zipper to her jeans. To his male satisfaction, her hands returned the favor, freeing his hard length from his confining jeans.

He sucked in a ragged breath when she slid her hand up and down the length of him.

"Don't. I'm too close," he groaned.

She didn't reply with words. Instead, she braced herself against him to stand. Reece stared at her wildly as he thought she meant to put a stop to their glorious lovemaking, but instead, she pushed her jeans down, baring a mound neatly trimmed and smelling gloriously of her arousal. Reece struggled to his knees, his mouth watering at the temptation she offered.

But again, she surprised him. She turned to give him her back and then bent over, exposing her pink core. She peered over her shoulder in a come-hither glance, all the invitation he needed.

He sprang up from the ground, his cock leading the way. He stood behind her and almost groaned at the height difference. But he wouldn't let something trivial like that stop him now. He wrapped an arm around her waist and, bending his knees, nudged her wet slit with the tip of his cock. She shuddered, and fresh, scalding moisture seeped from her sex and soaked the head of his shaft.

He tried to take it slow as he eased himself into her tight channel, retaining enough control to be wary of hurting her. However, the minx apparently had no such trepidation and rocked back against him, sheathing his cock into her heat.

Reece threw his head back and bit back the howl that wanted to burst free. Buried deep inside his woman—*my mate*—he discovered an ecstasy like no other. He wanted to take his time, draw out both their pleasure, but her keening cries tore through his control. How could he resist her mewling "Harder"?

He gave her what she begged for, pounding her fast and hard. Her rounded buttocks proved a delight to slap up against, soft and accommodating, a perfect cushion for his pushing. After a few strokes, he fought not to burst. A part of him remained aware enough to remind him that she needed to come first. He used his rough fingers to stroke her clit, and his mate, so responsive and sensual, with a scream that made him growl in satisfaction, climaxed. Her already tight channel squeezed him even closer as it quivered wetly around his rod. The howl he'd held in burst forth as he lost control and spurted hotly inside her, marking and claiming her as his, forever more.

Overwhelmed and awed at the experience, he suddenly wished he had the gift of flowery words to tell her what sang in his heart and mind. Instead, he spoke without words, wrapping both his arms around her still shuddering body.

Reality, an oftentimes cold, harsh mistress, intruded.

※

Teddy, basking in the afterglow of the most amazing sex ever, took a moment to realize the name she heard being shouted in the distance was her own.

Ah shit. I forgot about Georgie. She separated—with reluctance—her intimately entwined body with that of the wolf at her back. *My mate.*

As she righted her clothes, she couldn't look at him, embarrassment raising its head at their wild coupling out in the open. His low timbered "That was fantastic" didn't help and, instead, brought a blushing heat to her cheeks, a sign he must have caught, for he chuckled.

Dressed—if sticky and hot—Teddy began walking toward the frantic sound of her sister calling for her. A moment later, a large hand clasped hers, and she stumbled to a halt.

She turned startled eyes up to the man at her side. In the dark, his features appeared softer—of course, the sex might have had something to with that—and his lips curved into a sensual smile that made her heart thump oddly.

However, the more her body cooled, the more she regretted what had just happened. *How could I have lost control like that?* The even bigger dilemma was how to extricate herself. She licked her lips. "That's my sister. We can't let her find us like this," she whispered, remembering even in her frazzled state that sound carried far, especially when shifters were around to hear.

He arched a brow at her in surprise. "Like what?"

"Looking like we just had wild monkey sex outside," she hissed.

"But we did," he replied with a broad grin that made his straight white teeth flash in the darkness.

Teddy blew out a breath. "Listen. I realize we've got some stuff to sort out, but can't it wait until the morning? I'm supposed to be looking after my sister, not wandering around in the woods—" Teddy stammered to a halt, tongue-tied and unable to speak any further. Having a healthy sex life was one thing, talking about it quite another.

The man at her side sighed. "Fine. Go take care of your sister. You have tonight to explain because starting tomorrow morning—" He dropped his voice. "You're going to be all *mine*." He drew her close to him and planted a scorching, proprietary kiss on her lips that set her limbs trembling.

Then he let go. With a wicked smile, he ran off into the darkness, and Teddy resumed her stumbling walk toward the bar. She hadn't gone far when she ran into her sister and several of her cousins.

Georgie took one look at her face and pulled her aside to whisper, "What's wrong, Teddy? You look like you just ran a marathon."

Oh, I ran a race, all right. A race to the greatest climax ever. Teddy bit her tongue so as to not giggle. "I went for a jog trying to stay awake. I'm tired. Ready to go back to the motel?"

Georgie's brow creased. "Wait a second. What about your mate? I thought you said you found him in the bar."

"I was mistaken," Teddy lied, unable to admit she'd allowed the wolf, who thought her too fat, to screw her, and without a fight.

Teddy swung on her heel and headed toward their minivan, but her sister wasn't done and kept up a barrage of questions as she walked alongside.

"I don't understand. What do you mean you were mistaken? I was under the impression that, once you found him, there was no mistaking it."

"I guess my bear got confused."

"But—"

Teddy cut her sister off. "Listen. I'm tired, and I

think I'm coming down with something, which is probably why I thought I smelled something I didn't. I take it you didn't find your mate?" Teddy changed the subject in the hopes of shaking her sister and her inquisition.

Her sister shook her head. "Nope. Although I did get a lot of offers." Georgie's grin and wink made Teddy laugh. She pretended interest as her sister told her of the come-on lines she'd been subjected to, but while Teddy laughed and smiled in the right spots, her mind was focused on something else. Make that *someone* else.

She still wasn't sure why she'd lied to her sister. She'd let the man have sex with her after all—glorious, toe-curling sex. But now that she'd gotten away from him and his libido-disturbing presence, she couldn't help castigating herself.

How could I let him take me like that knowing he thinks I'm ugly and fat? Although he didn't seem to mind my extra curves once he got his hands on me, her insidious mind replied.

Teddy wanted to snort. She didn't find it a compliment that the only reason he'd taken her was because his beast and hormones had made him. If it hadn't been for those factors, he wouldn't have touched her with a ten-foot pole. And what about her, though? Mate or not, she'd allowed a perfect stranger—*I never even got his first name*—to seduce her out in the open. Teddy had no problem with one-night stands. When she chose them. But to allow a seduction by a man who'd blatantly admitted he didn't find her attractive? That went beyond stupid into shameful.

And if there was one thing Teddy wouldn't stand for, it was humiliation, even if the sex was out of this world. *I have to get out of here. First thing in the morning, I'm packing Georgie up and we're going back home.* Cowardly or not, she'd run because she refused and had too much pride to be with a man who thought she was less than perfect.

Decision made, she settled down to sleep beside her lightly snoring sister. She should have been pleased that she wouldn't allow herself to be used. But all the right reasons in the world didn't stop the trickle of tears that soaked her pillow. *What kind of cruel mistress is fate to give me the one man who doesn't think my curves are beautiful?*

CHAPTER 4

Reece couldn't sleep when he got home. His mind raced too wildly for that, filled with thoughts of his mate.

What a stroke of luck that I just got back from the north in time to meet her. Reece worked as an ice road trucker. A distinctly unglamorous job that didn't last long, but paid extremely well. With what he'd earned over the past few months and what he already had socked away, he could afford to take a few months off to get to know his soon-to-be wife—naked. *I can't wait to get her home so I can explore those curves and, even better, ride them.*

His lusty thoughts made his cock rise, but instead of jacking off to the remembrance of her moist heat, he went on a cleaning rampage. A much-needed endeavor, he realized, as he critically eyed his distinctly masculine space. When he brought his mate back to her new home, he didn't want her first impression to be that she'd hooked up with an animal, even if he'd taken her out in the open like a beast. Which reminded him, he should probably wash the sheets, lest she catch the scent of his last sexual encounter.

It was only as he shoved the sheets in the washer that he realized that not only did he not know where to find his mate in the morning they'd never even exchanged names.

I'm a fucking moron. He mentally castigated himself and didn't allow himself a reprieve, even as he duly noted they hadn't really talked much. Out loud, that was. Their bodies, though, they'd had quite the *conversation.*

Racking his brain and rerunning the evening's events, he realized he did know her name, ludicrous as it seemed. He'd heard it shouted by the blonde whom she claimed was her sister. *Teddy.*

No way is that her real name. It's probably some kind of childhood nickname. A play on words given she's a bear. One who, in his mind, appeared cuter and cuter. Sure, her short hair and stature, not to mention her rounded frame, had thrown him initially for a loop. But with the shock of meeting his mate wearing off, he could admit her bobbed cap of black hair with its blue sheen complemented her face with its spattering of freckles across the bridge of her nose. She also possessed amazing eyes, a blue so clear it made him think of a cloudless sunny sky out on the ice plains. Short and rounded, she still had an hourglass shape with a smaller waist than he'd expected. While he hadn't yet seen her naked in all her glory, he found himself looking forward to exploring her lush body. He'd definitely enjoyed the feel of her heavy breasts in his hands. And her bottom... Just remembering how its soft pillow had welcomed his thrusting body made him hard all over again.

His previous revulsion for women who carried around a few extra pounds was fading fast. Horny and now more eager than ever to reconnect with her, he worked like a madman preparing his home for his soon-to-be blushing—from arousal—bride.

The fact that she was a bear and not a wolf didn't bother him. Everyone in the shifter circles knew wolf genes were dominant when it came to pups. He almost froze as the idea of fathering his own litter hit him like a ton of bricks. Why, this time next year, he might join the ranks of boasting fathers in the pack. The concept, which would have probably sent him running to the ice fields a few days ago, didn't sound so horrid any more. *A son to carry on my name. Or a daughter to coddle.*

He whistled as he finished rearranging his space.

There wasn't much he could do about the décor, but he'd make it clear to her that she'd enjoy a free hand decorating, well, so long as she didn't go crazy with ruffles or girly pastel colors.

Only when he fell into bed, hours later, exhausted, did the nagging reminder that he still didn't know where to find her resurface. He batted the irritating thought away. Fate had brought them together once. Surely, she'd give them a hand reconnecting the next day.

Of course, he'd forgotten one important fact. Fate was a bitch.

REECE WOKE EARLY, catching only a few hours of sleep. Eagerness, though—and a few cups of coffee—made him energetic and ready to hunt down his woman. Hours later, staring at the empty motel room, which still held her lingering scent, he faced the shocking truth. *She left.*

Pride made him stalk back in a fury to his house, a case of beer tucked under one arm, the largest whiskey bottle he could find under the other. As a werewolf, getting drunk took an effort, and he gave it his best shot. He downed beer after beer in quick succession, trying to dull the inexplicable ache inside him and the irritable wolf that insisted he chase after her.

But a man had his pride, and he ignored both his own urges and that of his beast. *She's made it clear she doesn't want me. I don't care. It's not like I wanted her either.*

The alcohol slowly took effect, but instead of numbing his emotions and his body, they focused in even more intently on his missing woman.

Why did she leave? I gave her pleasure. I felt it all around my cock and heard it when she screamed. And yet, even knowing the delight he could give her, she'd fled. *Dammit, doesn't she realize we're meant to be together?* He wondered if she was, even now, wherever she'd run to, regretting her choice. Wouldn't that serve her right if she had to come crawling back? Of course, there was only one problem with that scenario. She had no idea who the fuck he was or where to find him.

Those two thoughts sobered him in an instant.

He sighed as he scrubbed his face. There was only one thing to do, whether his pride liked it or not. He'd have to go find her, and if she tried to refuse or run from him again, he had a plan. *I'll kidnap her hot ass, tie her up, and pleasure her until she realizes she can't live without me.*

Oh, and get her real bloody name, not to mention tell her mine, because next time she screams in pleasure, it's going to be my fucking name, and I'll make sure she yells it so many times she never forgets it or me.

⁂

Teddy already had their bags packed and in the minivan the next morning before her sister had even taken a bite of her breakfast. Her cousins decided to stay for a few extra days. So it was just Teddy and Georgie on that long ride home. Teddy kept the tunes cranked in the van in order to forestall the questions she could see in her sister's eyes. Only once they'd driven a few hours—while constantly checking the rearview mirror for signs of pursuit—did she breathe a sigh of relief, even as her heart plummeted and her bear settled down for a disgruntled nap.

Teddy was determined to return to her life and forget about the big, bad wolf who'd claimed her. *It's not like he actually liked or wanted me. It was only the damned mating hormones that made him touch me in the first place.*

She tried to blame her seduction by him on the same thing, but lying to herself failed miserably. Alone, she could admit that, while she hated his attitude and the fact that he made no bones about disliking plump women, she couldn't deny that he, on the other hand, was exactly what she liked in a man. *Although a little less height would have probably worked better.*

Her pussy still quivered each time she remembered the way he'd plowed her—satisfyingly deep and hard—with his thick cock. Her nipples tightened every time she remembered his mouth sucking at them while his hands fondled her breasts.

The smart thing to do would be to banish the ghost of his lovemaking.

Once she got home, she opened her black book of names several times, only to flip through it with disinterest. In the end, she flung it with a curse across the room.

The idea of sex with another man—*not my mate*—left her cold, and to her disgust, every time she brought it to mind, she felt dirty somehow, as if even the thought was cheating.

How can it be cheating when I don't even know the guy's name?

It had appalled her to realize on the long drive home that she didn't have the slightest inkling of who the hell he was. She didn't even know if he lived in the town she'd visited with her sister and cousins or if he, like them, was transient and looking for a mate—or a good time. She wondered what he thought of it all. Did he miss her, or had he breathed a sigh of relief he'd dodged a chubby bullet?

Teddy passed the days after her return on autopilot. She went to work at the school where she taught kindergarten then came home to an empty house. Hard as she tried, she couldn't forget the wolf. *Maybe I should have given him a chance.* Right on the heels of that thought was, *not in this lifetime.*

The several times Teddy talked to her mother, her mama, surprisingly enough, didn't say a word to her. Georgie had surely talked, and even without the full details, Teddy wondered how her usually nosy mother managed to hold her tongue.

Almost a week passed, and with each long, lonely day, Teddy's own resolve and decision weighed heavier on her. *Did I make the right choice? I'm not getting any younger, after all, and while I might not be his physical ideal, even he couldn't deny—nor can I—the sexual chemistry.* She'd also come to the shocking realization at one point during one of her sleepless nights that there was a possibility she even carried his pup. The idea both elated and terrified her.

The mature thing to do would have been to purchase a pregnancy test, but she lived in a small town. If she did that, it wouldn't take long before the whole town was talking about it and asking her where and who the father was.

Instead of facing the inquisition, she waited. In another five days, the appearance or not of her period would answer the question for her without the whole town weighing in.

How she'd deal with it was another matter. The idea of pregnancy should have sent her running for the woods, but she couldn't deny she wanted a child of her own. *But what of the father?*

A bridge she'd cross once she knew for certain one way or another.

Sunday arrived—a week and a day since her return, not that she was keeping count—and she drove to her mother's house for the traditional Sunday night dinner. She'd have preferred to stay home and mope, her newest pastime, but if there was one thing she didn't dare miss it was Mama's supper. Not unless she wanted her mama bear to hunt her down and tan her hide.

However, while she went, her appearance reflected her mood. She wore shapeless track pants and a stretched sweatshirt in dark colors that matched the circles under her eyes. If anyone asked, she could honestly state she hadn't been sleeping. However, it was more than likely, in the chaos that usually ensued weekly with her many nieces and nephews galloping about, she'd be able to slide in obscurity and bide her time until she could escape.

As she pulled up, she noticed a black Durango in the driveway. The gas-guzzler was spattered in mud as if it had driven cross country using the shortest route instead of highways. She idly wondered which distant relative had arrived for a visit.

Teddy entered her mother's home to familiar chaos. High-pitched squeals bounced around the room as Jaiden chased his cousin, Kevin. She winced as the noise washed over her, an overload of sound that reminded her loudly that, no matter her mood, life went on. A tug on her leg had her peering down with a smile and scooping up the toddler who raised chubby arms in demand.

"Hi, Beth." Teddy gave the little one a smacking kiss. Baby Beth replied with a really wet one of her own that had Teddy giggling, a laugh cut short as her nose twitched at an unexpected scent.

No way. She inhaled deeper, and amongst the familiar scents of home, mingled a new one that had no place here. Her bear chuffed happily in her mind, and her tummy went spinning. *He found me.*

Panic gripped her, even as her heart rate sped up in excitement. She became all too aware of her drab state of dress, not her most flattering look, for sure. She set the baby down and turned on her heel, preparing to flee.

A softly growled, "Don't you dare," from behind her froze her in her tracks. For a second. The next, she went flying out the door.

She heard an exasperated sigh, but caught in the grips of irrationality, she jumped off the porch to the ground. She took off running toward the woods, a familiar hideout of hers. She knew, even as her short legs pumped, she wouldn't win this race. And, even stranger, she wasn't sure she wanted to.

Not that she thought about it for long. A pair of arms that could rival the strongest steel wrapped around her from behind and lifted her with pedaling feet off the ground.

"Caught you," he whispered in her ear before he caught the lobe between his lips for a nibble.

CHAPTER 5

Frustrating as his week-long search for his missing Teddy bear ended up being—he'd had plenty of time to plan some titillating punishment for her when he caught her—all his irritation melted away when he saw her in her mother's living room, looking adorably disheveled, exchanging kisses with a baby. His heart stopped as he easily pictured her holding their own child, a thought that roused his heretofore-unknown possessive side. *My mate, my soon-to-be wife, and the future mother of my child.* He'd always wondered how he would feel when it came time to settle down and form a family pack of his own. To his surprise, he couldn't wait.

The moment she realized he'd found her was unmistakable. Her eyes widened, her face blanched, and she put down the baby she held in preparation for flight.

His "Don't you dare" had an opposite effect. Instead of his words challenging her to stay and face him, she leapt out the door and off the porch like a wannabe gazelle. With a sigh, and to the sound of chuckles from her family, he took off after her.

She had to know she couldn't outrun him. Hell, he didn't even have to jog. His longer stride caught him up to her easily, and when he plucked her heaving body, wrapping her securely in arms that would never again let her go, he couldn't resist teasing her. "Caught you." He followed up his words with a bite on her ear lobe. However, he hadn't counted on his body and wolf's reaction to finding and touching her again. Instant arousal made him rock hard, and when she stropped struggling and sighed in his embrace, he wanted to strip her naked and take her right there.

Of course, her mama might have an issue with that. Even Reece wasn't brazen enough to challenge a mother bear. He'd first met the formidable matriarch when she'd come up to him in town and, with a cold glint in her eye, demanded to know why he was looking for her daughter, Teddy.

He'd quite enjoyed the look on the mama's bear's face when he'd announced Teddy—short, he'd discovered, for Theodora—was his mate.

Instead of telling him where to find her, she'd told him to show up at her house on Sunday for dinner with the family. Somehow, the expression on her face tied his tongue when he would have demanded she tell him where Teddy hid. Reece had spent the time since Friday in a state of anxiety and eagerness.

And now, the wait was over, and he held her. Soft and plush, her womanly curves were a perfect fit for his arms. He couldn't resist nuzzling the soft skin of her nape and inhaling her fragrance, one that made his eyes widen in surprise. *No way.* He didn't have time to ponder his revelation because his mate demanded answers.

"How did you find me?" she gasped.

"I followed my nose," he said when, in reality, simple instinct had guided him after all his attempts to find her through traditional methods had failed. He still wasn't sure how he'd known where to go, but he thanked fate for showing him the way.

"Teddy, if you're done playing hard to get, would you mind bringing your swain inside for dinner?"

Reece heard the order in the mama bear's request, and so did Teddy. She sagged in his arms and meekly said, "We'd better go in before she comes back out with the wooden spoon."

He set her on her feet and turned her around so she faced him. Well, she did after he tilted her chin up and forced her eyes to meet his. "Before we go inside, it's long past we did this. My name, by the way, is Reece."

A ghost of a smile hovered on her lips. "I guess that means I can't call you dog anymore then."

"Call me whatever you like, but keep in mind, I do retaliate, Teddy bear."

Her eyes widened, and she opened her mouth to retort, but he quickly lifted her and kissed her soft mouth before anything scathing emerged. When he felt he'd addled her enough—a state he could judge by his own befuddled mind—he set her back down and, tucking her hand into his, tugged her back in the direction of her home.

Dinner should be interesting. He looked forward to discovering her family and Teddy's childhood secrets, but truthfully, he found himself much more interested in tasting the dessert at his side. He did so love sweet pussy pie.

I'M DREAMING. There could be no other explanation, she thought as she let Reece lead her back into her house to face the curious and amused stares of her family.

While the kids ran around as if nothing had happened, the adults all fell silent at their reappearance, and Teddy blushed at their rapt attention.

Reece, the jerk, appeared unperturbed. He raised a big hand and waved. "Hi, folks. My name is Reece Peterson. I'm a wolf from the Pelly River pack in the Northwest Territories. I work as an ice road trucker, and in my spare time I like to camp, ski, and, more recently, drive Teddy nuts."

Her family's laughter at his speech made her blush only harder, as well as fervently wish for the ground to open up and swallow her whole. Thankfully, she didn't have to reply because her mother banged her wooden spoon off the wall, and everyone moved to the table.

Teddy ended up crammed in beside Reece's hard body as the large table brimmed to overflowing. It appeared her mama had invited—AKA threatened— everyone to get their hairy butts over to gawk at Teddy and the giant wolf who appeared determined to claim her as his.

"Teddy, shouldn't you introduce your family to your mate?" Her mother posed it as a question, but Teddy heard the order.

With a sigh, she obeyed. One by one, she pointed out her sisters and their husbands. "That's my sister, Jamie, and her husband, Frank. Lyndie and Joe. Geraldine and Mike. Frankie and Bill. And my baby sister, Georgie. Before you ask, Mama is from the

American Rocky tribe, and even though she relocated to the Canadian side, she insisted on naming us after her favorite U.S. presidents."

Reece's jaw dropped, and then he laughed, a deep, rich sound that was joined by that of her family, not that she paid them mind. How could she when her entire body shivered in arousal? Talk about the wrong place and time to get horny.

She wasn't quite paying attention to his words, more concerned with getting her libido under control. She took a drink of water and then choked as what he said penetrated. "I think that's a fine tradition, but given my Canadian heritage, I think Teddy and I shall name our children after Canadian premieres."

She coughed, and her eyes watered as her drink went down the wrong pipe. Reece, his eyes alight with laughter, rubbed her back as she wheezed. When her fit subsided, she glared at him, but the unrepentant dog just grinned. He leaned in to whisper in her ear. "Just so you know, I'm really looking forward to making those babies."

Heat made her cheeks flush, and she dropped her gaze, lest anyone—most especially him—see that it wasn't embarrassment lighting her skin but desire at the erotic image his words suddenly painted in her mind.

Dinner went on, and she didn't understand how

he could sit and converse as if nothing was wrong. He seemed perfectly at ease. He talked and laughed with her family as if he'd known them for years, and yet she couldn't complain he ignored her because her big dog—more housetrained than she'd initially given him credit for—kept a possessive hand on her thigh, and he squeezed it often. That, mixed with the smiles he kept bestowing on her, frazzled her already shot nerves.

When dinner ended and her mama stood to begin clearing, Teddy shot up too, quickly grabbing an armful of plates and following her mama into the kitchen. Once there, she stayed, hiding like a chicken.

Her mother eyed her as she stacked the heavy-duty dishwasher. "So, you found your mate on your trip, eh?"

Teddy bit her lip and nodded. The dreaded conversation had arrived, and she didn't know what to say. Her mother was a firm believer in the mating bond, even given her own experience had ended up less than stellar. She would never understand why Teddy refused to follow what fate ordained. *How can I explain to her that I want more than just a chemical pairing? Is it so wrong to want love, real love?*

"Care to explain why he had to come looking for you?"

Teddy didn't think she could voice her reasons

aloud, so she shook her head wildly instead, sending her short hair flying.

"It's my fault." His deep baritone made her legs tremble, and she held on to the counter, not daring to turn and look at him. *I'll probably melt into a puddle if I do.* Like, love, or not, the sizzling heat and tension between them refused to give her a choice. She ignored him and her body's urges.

"Explain," said her mama in a voice that had caused more than one reluctant cub to spill all.

"I'm afraid that I didn't react too well when I first met Theodora. Actually, you could say I behaved like an ignorant ass."

Teddy couldn't believe his admission, and she cringed as she waited for her mother to lambaste him for his conduct. But apparently, today was to be one of surprises.

"And now?"

"I intend to make it up to her and prove to her that I'm very happy with the mate fate's chosen for me."

And there it was. He hadn't shown up because he wanted her. He'd come because it was what shifters did when they found their mate, an uncontrollable urge that made them pair up with someone, even if that someone wasn't who or what they wanted.

It roused her anger, which, in turn, bolstered her courage. "Don't I get a say in this?" Teddy turned to face both her mother and Reece with pursed lips. "Has it occurred to anyone that maybe I don't want to spend my life with a man who thinks I'm ugly just because some weird mystical crap says he has to?"

"I never said you were ugly," he snapped.

"No, you said I was chubby and not your type," she retorted. "Well, guess what. You're not my type either. I wanted a bear for a mate, not a grizzly, old wolf. And you're…you're too tall." With that lame comeback, she spun on her heel, stalked back out into the living room and right out the front door. She ignored her car and stripped as she ran across the front lawn, her mother's remote location making it unlikely any humans would see her. Her bear burst free from the human skin confining it, and with a disgusted snort, Teddy lumbered into the woods.

Her reaction to run away, while immature, was one ingrained from childhood. It stemmed from a time when the other children would taunt her about her weight and, when she got older, her short stature. And yet, when it came to anything else, she held her ground and would argue until she turned blue. Even odder was she thought she'd gotten over her fleeing years. Once she'd reached adulthood, she'd come to grips with the fact that she'd never have the body of a svelte model, and she'd also discovered that many men didn't care if she had a few extra pounds. Heck, they loved them. So why did she keep allowing one ill-bred wolf to make her feel bad about her size? *Who cares what he thinks? I'm beautiful, and I don't need him to make me feel good about my body.* But as much as she repeated this mantra to herself, she just couldn't forget their first meeting and the look in his eyes when he'd seen her. Nor could she escape the fear that if she did forgive him, he'd betray her.

The mating bond brought shifters together, made them crazy in lust for each other. However, once the male got a cub from the female, in other words, made her pregnant, the hormones that drove them to copulate wildly faded. And that was when some of the males strayed. Her own father had done it to her mother until he'd died in an accident, and when Teddy tried to ask her mother, the strongest woman she knew, why she put up with it, she'd replied, "He's my mate." As answers went, it sucked. Not to mention, Teddy craved more. Without a bond of love, Teddy feared she'd end up one of those hollow-eyed women who put on a brave face. Heck. It was what her sister, Lyndie, did each time she got pregnant. Teddy had asked once why she didn't leave him. Lyndie smiled at her and said, "Because, as soon as that baby is born, he's mine again." And since the birth of their fourth child, Lyndie had kept things that way by the use of a secret IUD.

But Teddy wanted more out of a relationship

than her sister. She wanted a love that lasted through pregnancy and not. *My other sisters have that kind of love,* her irritating conscience reminded her. *Yeah, but their husbands thought they were pretty from day one. Wait until I'm pregnant and really chubby. No way will he stick around.* Teddy didn't think she could survive the heartbreak of having a mate who strayed.

So she ran. Away from her family who wouldn't understand. Away from the man who wanted to make her forget her promises to herself. And, most of all, she ran away from the pain she was sure he'd bring.

She could never count the passing of time when she became her beast, but she noted the deepening shadows as night crept over the land. She made her way with a lumbering gait toward home. Much as she hated the situation fate had thrown at her, she could run for only so long. A braver, more intrepid bear would have kept going, away from everyone and everything. But Teddy, much as they might not understand her, loved her family. She'd just have to be strong against the pressure and not cave to their demands and that of the man who'd come to claim her.

She emerged from the forest right into her backyard. She shifted back to her human shape, her remote home far from prying human eyes. She'd almost reached her rear sliding door when a prickle along the back of her neck informed her she had company. She whirled and crouched in a defensive posture, only to relax when she saw what approached.

From the woods slunk a massive wolf, his thick fur a deep brown. Above the long muzzle peered familiar eyes. It bared teeth at her in a version of a canine smile, and its tongue lolled.

Teddy rolled her eyes. "Why won't you just go away?"

The large wolf's body shrank and contorted back into that of her pain-in-the-ass mate. A very naked mate. She sucked in a breath as her pussy soaked at the sight of all his rippling muscles and his very erect cock. *Why does he have to be so damned scrumptious?*

She planted her hands on her hips, aware of her nudity but too annoyed to hide it. Besides, shifters didn't have hang-ups about nakedness like humans did. Not to mention, maybe if he saw, in glaring color, her full-figured size, he'd do them both a favor and run back home. If his cock was any judge, though, the mating urge was still overpowering his dislike of chubby women. "Did you follow me?"

"Every step of the way," he said with an unrepentant grin as he strode toward her.

Teddy tried to hold on to her anger but found it damned hard with six-feet-plus of virile male stalking toward her, the sexual intent in his eyes matching his raging erection.

"I didn't smell you," she said, suddenly wishing she had another pairs of arms to cross over chest to hide her tightening nipples.

"I'm a wolf, Teddy bear. I'm good at hiding. I've been following you since you took off from your mama's. And, might I say, your bear has a very naughty wiggle."

"You're a dog," she said with a shake of her head while an unbidden smile tugged at her lips.

"I prefer the term big, bad wolf. Now, are you going to invite me in so we can talk, or am I just going to claim your sweet body outside again?"

Teddy's legs went weak with arousal as her mind painted a vivid picture of him holding her up against her sliding glass door as he plowed her. Moisture pooled in her cleft.

He uttered a soft growl as he brought her mental fantasy partially to life. His hands spanned her waist, and he raised her with ease. The cold glass of the door pressed against her back, but she welcomed the coolness because her body was on fire.

His hard lips met hers in a fiery kiss that stole her breath and good intentions. She knew where this was going, knew she'd regret it later, but she couldn't find the will to push him away. Heck, she drew him closer by wrapping her arms around his neck and her legs around his waist.

I already know I'm going to castigate myself for this later, so I might as well make the most of it now.

She embraced him back, slipping her tongue into his mouth, a quiver of excitement shooting through her when he grumbled with pleasure. While their mouths meshed in a wet, intimate kiss, his hands somehow moved from her waist to cup her full bottom, an interesting position that left his bobbing cock just under her cleft.

The way he held her, so effortlessly in his palms, made her feel dainty and sexy. It was also utterly decadent and unheard of, for her at least.

She tore her lips from his only to nibble her way across his bristled jaw to his ear lobe. She sucked that tender piece of flesh in her mouth, and he groaned. Then she bit him.

He moaned even louder.

She'd meant to grab his attention with her bite, and she got it all right, right between the thighs. He took her bite as an urging for more. She vaguely recalled that she had reasons she should protest his sensual probing of her cleft with his prick, but she ignored those irritating thoughts in favor of concentrating on his thick cock penetrating her wet slit. When he teased her, instead of impaling her right away, she bit him again.

His breathing grew even more ragged, and his mouth found the skin of her neck. His bristle chafed sensually against her skin, and she squeaked when he nibbled her back, all the while filling her with his shaft in long, steady strokes.

Words failed her, and she could only moan, helplessly caught in the grips of overwhelming bliss. While she couldn't express what she needed, her body, trembling in his grasp, said it all.

His fingers dug into her cheeks as he slammed his shaft home over and over again. Teddy cried out, her whole body taut with desire. She gripped him even tighter with her own fingers, leaving marks for sure on the skin of his back and shoulders. But the louder she keened and clawed at him, the harder he pistoned her channel, the slick friction bringing on her orgasm lightning quick.

Teddy wailed with the intensity of it, her body convulsing in waves of pleasure that left her limp. He shouted, himself, when he found his relief buried inside of her, triggering a smaller orgasm that almost made her sob with the painful ecstasy of it.

How long they stood out there in the chill evening air, bodies intimately wrapped together, she couldn't tell. All she knew was she'd never felt so satisfied, so complete.

She thought of protesting when he slid open the door to her house and carried her in, all the while maintaining their intimate joining. She managed to open her eyes finally when he dropped her on her mattress.

Teddy stared up at him with heavy-lidded eyes, her mind still befuddled from the passion they'd shared. The expression on his face was fierce and possessive. It made her tremble with longing and reignited her desire. Then she saw his eyes flick down to look at her body, and reality came rudely crashing back.

"You need to go," she stated as she drew her comforter around to hide her body before his eyes assumed the look of disgust she'd seen before. *I don't think I could bear it, not after what just happened.*

His brow furrowed. "I am not leaving. You're my mate."

"And you mated me. Happy? Now go. I am not sharing my bed with a hairy dog." She used insults to hasten his departure because, every moment he stayed, her resolve weakened.

His eyes narrowed, and a tic formed on the side of his jaw. "Why must you insist on fighting me, Teddy bear? I'm not going away. The sooner you realize that, the better."

"Says the man acting under the influence of his hormones. Don't worry. You'll eventually see I'm right. As soon as you knock me up, which, given the fact you haven't used protection, should be anytime now, you'll come to your senses and leave." Saying the words aloud killed her arousal, and aching sorrow crept into her heart.

"I don't cheat." He said the words vehemently, and she wanted to believe him, but she had only to remember her poor sister and mother to know how easily promises were broken.

"You also don't like plump women," she retorted. "I want more from a mate than great fucking until he gets me pregnant." The vulgar word she used hung in the air, and she almost felt dirty for having used it to describe their incredible coupling.

"What do you want from me?" he bit out, his anger palpable as he stood there, still naked with his hands clenched into fists at his side.

"Nothing you can give me." Teddy rolled onto her side and gave him her back. She couldn't face him anymore, not with the hot tears that spilled from her eyes.

She shouldn't have been surprised when he left without a further fight, but she sobbed anyway. *I wish I could believe him. Trust him. But if my poor sister, who's slim and pretty, can't keep her mate from straying, then what chance do I have?*

CHAPTER 6

Reece raced through the woods back to Teddy's parents' house. Anger fought with bafflement. *Why does she keep rejecting me?*

He'd thought for sure, given her enthusiastic response to his lovemaking at her house, that she'd finally abandoned her stubborn stance. But instead, she'd lashed out and pushed him away. He'd left, even as he wanted to gather her up in his arms and hug her. He'd smelled her tears when she gave him her back, sensed her misery, and it killed him to know he was the cause. *I haven't done anything wrong, and yet she acts like I have. What's it going to take to get through to her? To make her realize I'm here to stay?*

He understood his initial attraction had come about because of the mating bond, but the more he got to know her, the more she drew him. When he'd emerged earlier from the woods and seen her standing there like a naked goddess in the starlight, he'd chastised himself for ever thinking she appeared less than perfect. Yes, she had a lush frame, but instead of finding it repugnant, it made her more desirable. Her shape just seemed more womanly, from her full breasts to her indented waist, her rounded, soft belly and flaring hips. She was perfection. *Mine.*

He couldn't believe that she thought he'd leave the moment she got pregnant. Sure, this overwhelming need to touch her and be with her would tone down as they settled into life as a couple, but to jump from that to the erroneous conclusion that he'd cheat on her? Reece howled his frustration aloud.

Never. Reece might have played many roles in his life, but a cheater wasn't one of them. His mad dash through the woods brought him to the edge of the forest where he'd initially stripped to chase after Teddy. His clothes still lay in an untidy pile ,and he shifted back to his human shape so he could pull them on. Long strides took him across the front lawn toward his parked truck.

A voice called him from the porch. "Is she still being stubborn?"

Teddy's mama, Annette, sat on a rocking chair,

and Reece, needing answers, went to sit with her. "I don't understand why she's fighting me. Us," he admitted, hating how lost he sounded. *Some big, bad wolf I am. Brought down by a little bear.*

For a moment, the only sound was the creaking of the chair as Annette rocked. "Teddy had a hard time growing up. You might have noticed Teddy looks a little different from the rest of us. She's an offshoot from her grandmother's side, where the bears were smaller and chubbier. Growing up, she had to put up with a lot of teasing and bullying over the fact she was smaller and not as slim as the rest of the pack."

"I've apologized for my initial reaction," he protested, even as he cringed that, at their first meeting, he'd unwittingly caused Teddy to recall the bullying of her youth. *And since then, I've shown her with my body how wrong I was.*

"Oh, I'm sure you have. But there's more to it than her carrying a painful chip on her shoulder because of her stature. Teddy's afraid of being hurt. She's seen several of her friends, and even her sister, suffer because their mates have strayed. Even though she wasn't aware of it at the time, she also came to discover that her own papa had a problem staying true." Annette sighed sadly. "Teddy's fragile love of herself couldn't handle having her mate stray on her, especially not with a woman she perceives as prettier than her."

"But she's beautiful."

"Is she now?" Annette's voice mocked him. "That wasn't your first reaction, though, remember? And before you argue, I know you've changed your mind since then. She, however, is terrified, once she gets pregnant, you'll change your mind and hurt her. It's why she keeps running."

"But she's already pregnant, dammit, and it hasn't changed my thoughts. I still think she's gorgeous, and I have no intention of going anywhere."

Annette gave him a sharp look. "How do you know she's with child?"

Reece shrugged. "I've got a good sense of smell. I noticed it when we reunited outside before dinner. I've been around enough pregnant women because of my packmates to know their scent changes. So her fears are groundless. I'll just tell her, and she'll have to believe me."

Annette laughed. "Oh, you poor puppy. You can't do that. She'll run before she listens."

Reece sighed. Why couldn't anything ever be simple? "So how do I prove to her that, pregnant or not, I'm here to stay?"

"Time. Show her while she gets big and round with your child that you care, and eventually, she'll accept you."

Reece rubbed his face. "I don't know if I can wait that long. I want to be with her now."

"Is it truly her you want, or is it your wolf and pride overriding your normal judgment with instinct?"

Reece thought of Teddy, the way her eyes flashed with defiance. The way her lips tilted when she tried not to smile. How she clung to him when he pleasured her. How right she felt cradled in his arms. "I want her, stubborn little minx that she is."

"Then show her. And not just with your body, puppy. Show her that you want her for her mind and heart, too."

"But how?" In the past, his relationships had never gone further than the bedroom. How could he show her he cared about her without the sex?

"Get to know her. Listen to her. Find out what makes her tick. Discover each other, with clothes on."

Reece pondered the mama bear's words as he drove through the winding roads back to Teddy's place. He mused them as he broke through Teddy's flimsy locks to gain entrance to her home. They echoed in his head as he stared down at Teddy, huddled in her bed, her cheeks still tear-stained. He turned the suggestions over in his mind as he bunked down on Teddy's couch.

If becoming Teddy's friend was how to get her to

realize they were fated as mates, then he'd become the best friend she ever had.

As for keeping our clothes on, good luck with that. Even I'm not strong enough to resist her hot and luscious body.

CHAPTER 7

The alarm went off, and Teddy groaned as she slapped at the annoying clock. She'd managed to fall asleep after crying herself dry. She'd kept trying to convince herself that pushing Reece away was the best decision for her and her bear, but in the light of day, her arguments looked as sheer as her curtains.

I wish I could believe him. But she had only to look in the mirror and know that she wasn't the type of woman to enjoy a fairytale ending.

She stumbled to her bathroom. She needed a hot shower to wake her up and erase the traces of their frantic lovemaking from the night before. The bathroom filled with steam, but even though she scrubbed her skin with soap, she couldn't erase his scent. It tickled her nose and made her cleft throb.

"Stupid dog," she muttered as she turned off the tap. She yanked the shower curtain back and screamed as a towel was draped around her.

"I'm delighted to see you, too," Reece said with a smile that should come with a warning. It certainly set off alarm bells in her pussy, the five-alarm, house-on-fire type.

Teddy shrieked. He grinned. She gaped at him, speechless, as he wrapped her securely in a towel and then scooped her up. "Put me down," she protested halfheartedly.

"Okay." He dropped her onto the bed, where she bounced, causing the towel to unravel. She should have ordered him out at that point. Covered herself up. Done something other than lick her lips and stare at him. For his part, he didn't touch her—the jerk. Instead, he stood staring down at her with a ghost of a smile about his lips.

"Breakfast is ready," he announced.

And then, the dratted dog turned on his heel and left.

Flustered—not to mention horny—Teddy scrambled into her clothes, a glance at the clock telling her she had just enough time to eat before she was due at school.

She dashed down the stairs and skidded to a halt at the entrance of her small kitchen. She rubbed her eyes, sure she must still be dreaming, but when she blinked and peeked again, she found Reece, looking perfectly at home, sliding plates with steaming food onto her round kitchen table.

She slid into a chair across from him and still couldn't find words, so she shoveled food into her mouth to give herself time to think.

He ate as if he didn't have a care in the world, but she could see mirth dancing in his eyes. *What does he think is so funny?* She saw nothing amusing with the knowledge he'd obviously broken in. She also didn't find any humor in the fact that he'd managed to resist her body. *See, it's already happening.*

Hunger didn't make her eat more food than she needed; hesitation did. *Why won't he go away?*

He broke the silence. "Ready for me to drive you to work?"

Teddy frowned. "I can drive myself."

"If you had a car. You left it at your mom's, remember?"

She did, unfortunately. Teddy glared at him. "I don't like you."

"Don't make me prove you're a liar, Teddy bear," he taunted, coming out of his seat. He leaned down in front of her, his dark eyes intent on her, his lips an inch away, and…scooped up her plate.

She gaped at his broad back as he washed the dishes, whistling a jaunty tune. Annoyed—and even hornier—Teddy finished getting ready to go, which involved mostly a lot of deep breathing and a pep talk about not mauling his smug mouth with her own.

They exited her home like some sort of married couple going off to work, and Teddy clenched her teeth at how right it felt. He held open the door to his truck, and when she hesitated at the height, he grabbed her around the waist and set her on the seat. Awareness of him flared immediately to life, and she sucked in a breath. He slammed the door shut and, a moment later, slid in on the driver's side. She fisted her hands in her lap and tried not to look at him, but her eyes kept straying. Since she couldn't seem to fight the allure of his presence, she forced herself to focus on an innocuous part of his body. She chose his hand on the gearshift. A big, capable hand filled with the strength to hold her up and callused digits perfect for… She wrenched her mind away from its naughty direction. Too late.

Heat pooled in her cleft, a wet longing that made her grit her teeth. She heard him growl.

"Stop that right now, you minx, or I will pull this truck over and make you late for work."

Startled, she looked sideways at him. His eyes met hers, and a moment later, with the spraying of gravel, the truck slammed to a stop and she was in his arms.

They devoured each other as if they were starving, their lips pressing together so hard their teeth clashed. And the taste of him, it made her moan low in her throat.

It was the honking of a passing vehicle that brought her back to her senses.

"Work," she panted as she pushed at him. "I need to get to work."

His eyes, alight with desire, made her want to retract her words, but without a word of protest—or attempt to resume their embrace—he resumed driving while Teddy fought to rediscover her composure. A lost cause with him sitting so temptingly close.

When they arrived at the school where she taught, she didn't wait for him. She opened the door and hopped out of the truck.

He leaned over the seat, and his gaze transfixed her as she prepared to swing the door shut.

"I'll pick you up at three thirty. Think of me, Teddy bear." He winked, and before she could throw herself back in the truck and his arms, she slammed the door shut.

Bemused, she watched him drive away. *What the heck just happened?*

The wolf was slick. She didn't know how, but he kept maneuvering her to do what he wanted, although, if she were truthful, she hadn't exactly fought him or even protested much.

It would serve him right if I found my own way home. Her obstinate side argued she should call her parents' house and have her car brought over. Then, with a vehicle at hand, she should claim she was sick and leave early, thus foiling his devious plot to pick her up and subject her to his annoyingly hot and sexy presence.

She did none of those things. Instead, she spent the day in a state of anticipation, waiting for it to end. When she dismissed the kids at three o'clock, she couldn't stop eagerness from flooding her. She tried to keep her hands and mind busy, but the minutes crawled by.

At three ten, awareness tickled her nape, and she whirled to see Reece standing in the doorway to her classroom. She almost gasped in surprise. She would have liked a little more time to prepare herself yet received no warning from the office that they'd let him in. In her small town, everyone still left their doors mostly unlocked, even their school. She hoped that never changed because she loved the fact she didn't have to walk through a metal detector each day. With the amount of wire she had in her bras, she'd set the thing off for sure.

Standing across the school, he watched her, his expression dark and enigmatic, she almost wondered at what he thought. Then he let her know the direction of his mind because there was no denying the sensual smile he sent her way was pure panty wetting sex.

"You're early," she stated, sounding cool, even if her heart raced.

"I couldn't wait to see you."

And it was claims like that which made him so dangerous because, even knowing how bad he was for her, she couldn't help for a moment believing him. Even worse, she enjoyed it.

She forced herself to stand her ground and not run to him like she longed to. Her refusal to yield could have led to a stalemate, but apparently, he didn't have the same issues she did. He came to her, his long-legged stride that of a predator who'd caught scent of his prey. She didn't resist, even as she knew she should, when he wrapped her in his arms for a hug. Instead, she caved to temptation and sighed when he dropped a hard kiss on her lips. *Oh, how I wish things could be different. What I wouldn't give for this to happen every day.*

He stepped back, his arms looped loosely around her. "Ready to go?"

Teddy could only stare at him blankly. "Go where?" Back to her place for hot sex? The back seat of his truck for scorching nookie? The broom closet for fumbling fun?

"Shopping, dinner, then a movie. Come on."

He folded her smaller hand in his, his fingers

lacing around hers, and pulled her along behind him while she tried to make sense of his actions—or lack thereof.

Why isn't he mauling me? Has he lost interest in me already? She might not have understood the game he played, but her body knew it didn't like it one bit.

※

Much as it killed him to not push her up against the nearest wall and take her, Reece held back. For now.

But dammit, she made it so damned hard. He'd arrived well before three, the longest he could stand waiting to see her. Once the bell rang at three o'clock, he'd paced around his truck, ignoring the interested looks of the women who'd come to fetch their children.

Only one woman held his attention, and although he called himself all kinds of pathetic pussy-whipped names, he couldn't keep himself from seeking her out before the allotted time. *So much for staying strong and not allowing a woman to control my actions.* He consoled himself with the fact that the prize would be well worth the loss of a little pride.

He'd no sooner caught sight of her, looking sweet and cuddly as she stretched to wipe the blackboard, than she sensed him. His heart thudded in his chest when her eyes lit up with eagerness, and although she didn't run to him, instinct told him she fought an inner battle not to. Unlike her, he didn't allow stubbornness to restrain him, and only when he held her in his arms—her pillowy curves a perfect fit—did he feel content. Awareness of where they were prevented him from kissing her deeply—and stripping her to love every inch of her body. Barely.

In the long hours they'd spent apart, he'd found the time, though, to return to speak with Teddy's mother and, even better, a pair of her sisters. They'd given him insight into his mate, and armed with information, he felt better prepared to seduce her mind and heart. He'd try and do as her mother and sisters advised. Take her out on real dates and get to know her—in public places where he had to behave. But once he got her home, her pussy was his, good intentions or not.

He had to admit that her reaction to his change of tactics amused him. Her eyes had a glassy sheen to them, and he could smell her arousal. Of course, the inverse problem was that, in the close confines of his truck, her scent drove him wild. It took an effort not to park the truck and quench his sexual thirst.

He battled his desire and, with his jaw rigid, drove them to the downtown strip, where he parked. He moved quickly and arrived in time to help down her from the truck—and cop a feel. He let her slide slowly down the front of him. Probably not his brightest idea, given his straining erection, but well worth the way she swayed against him. He dropped a light kiss on her lips, all he dared, and tucked her hand into his.

They strolled the storefronts in silence until they reached the display for the jeweler. He stopped, and she went a step or two before her hand, anchored in his, yanked her to a stop.

Her glance flicked to the storefront, widened, and then darted to him. He pretended not to notice and leaned in close. "See anything you like?"

She shook her head violently, sending her short strands of hair swinging. Reece arched a brow at her. He already knew she lied. Her sisters had kindly informed him which ring she had her eye on. A ring he'd already bought and would, in a few days, present to her once the jeweler sized it.

He didn't push her to answer. Instead, he started walking again and took her shopping for essentials. He could have technically done so while she taught, but it occurred to him that seeing him shop for items that indicated he wasn't going anywhere would perhaps start breaking through this erroneous wall of assumption she'd erected that made her believe his presence in her life was a passing phase.

He bought everything in bulk, and with each item he placed in the cart, he saw the questions mount in her eyes. It wasn't until they'd paid for their purchases and he'd piled them in his truck that she blurted out, "Are you planning on going somewhere?"

"Nope. I'm quite happy where I am."

His answer confused her, and her brow creased.

He leaned in and gave her a lazy smile. "It just occurred to me that, when you finally give in and realize I'm serious about being with you, that we might end up involved in a sex marathon and I wouldn't want us to run out of essentials."

He couldn't stop his laughter as her cheeks burned crimson.

"Jerk." She muttered the expletive, but Reece could tell she struggled not to join his mirth. She yanked her hand from his and stalked away with a wiggle that dried his laughter up and sent his blood shooting south.

"Where are you going?" he called when he realized she wasn't stopping.

She pivoted and faced him with a mischievous smile that went well with her twinkling eyes. A smile that took his breath away and shot a jolt of desire straight to his cock. In a too-sweet voice, she said, "Well, if you're planning to stay for a bit, then I'd better pick up more dog food and maybe some flea spray."

Reece roared with laughter. *Damn me, but I lucked out. Sexy and funny, too.*

⁂

Teddy couldn't help herself. She joined him giggling. Despite herself, she liked the jerk. And if it weren't for the whole I'm-your-mate thing, she would have thought he liked her, too. It was also obvious she wasn't going to easily get rid of him. It scared her to realize that, despite herself, she was falling for him. She wanted to stay aloof, but he made it impossible, not to mention her own mind and body kept betraying her. What surprised her was her bear was keeping quiet on the matter. But then again, her inner sow didn't have to push for her to mate with the jerk, seeing as how she couldn't seem to stop herself from indulging.

She allowed him to escort her to the restaurant then blushed as she noticed the eyes of all the shifters in the place, many of them related to her somehow, turning to watch them. Reece, with his hand in the middle of her back, led her to a table and seated her, a courteous gesture that tore down another brick in her wall of indifference.

Their outdoor mirth had loosened the tension between them, making conversation flow better than she would have expected. They ordered and, as they waited for their food, talked, a change from their usual arguments and torrid coupling.

He asked her about her childhood growing up as a cub. She glossed over some of her less-than-stellar moments, only to open up later when they ate. How could she not when he related how he'd lost both his parents in a hunting accident when he was still a pup? He spoke of his orphaning nonchalantly, but she caught the pain in his eyes, and on an impulse, she reached over the table and placed her hand on his in a gesture of comfort.

Electricity sizzled, and she met his eyes, drawn to them like metal to a lodestone. "I'm sorry." Trite words, but all she could manage to utter.

"Don't be. It was a long time ago. And besides, my grandmother made sure I had all the love I needed. She's going to really like you. I can't wait for you to meet her."

Teddy opened and shut her mouth, wanting to protest that would never happen, but not wanting to ruin the moment, she held her tongue.

They finished dinner, and with his hand back in the middle of her back—a hot brand she felt through her clothes—they went back to his truck. He helped her in, his hands lingering on her waist, and Teddy's pulse raced.

They went to the movies, and Teddy welcomed the darkness of the theater, where she could somewhat lose herself in the drama on screen. However, the storyline failed to grip her. All she could think about was how Reece sat next to her, his big thigh brushing against hers, his arm draped over her shoulder with fingers lazily tracing patterns on her shoulder. She peered sideways at him and found him not even attempting to pretend he watched the screen. He leaned over and kissed her.

Already aroused, a state she hadn't managed to shed since he'd arrived to pick her up, she responded instantly and eagerly. Her mouth opened under his to start a wet tongue duel.

It was crazy. Insane. So hot. Teddy vaguely realized they were in a public place, even if it was three quarters empty. But the knowledge, instead of dowsing her desire, enflamed it. She retained enough lucidity to remember to bite her tongue instead of crying out when his hand moved from around her shoulders to rest on her thigh. His fingers inched the fabric of her dress up, and Teddy closed her eyes at the tickling anticipation. When his hand reached her mound, covered by thin, wet silk, she couldn't hold back the sigh that escaped her lips. Slowly, he rubbed her cleft through the fabric, circular motions that made her tremble. Needing distraction, she flung her hand out to the side and groped at him. She, too, stroked her way up the firmness of his thigh. She reached the prominent bulge at his groin and rubbed.

Not to be outdone, he tore her panties, the sound of ripping fabric barely audible over the soundtrack of the movie, but thunderclap loud to Teddy. She opened her mouth to tell him to stop, sudden awareness making her mortified at what they were doing.

But his lips stifled her protest and caught her mewling cry as he inserted two fingers into her channel while his thumb rubbed at her clit. Teddy almost bit his tongue as she shook at the pleasure he wrung from her, a bliss amplified by the fact that she couldn't touch him skin to skin or cry her ecstasy out loud. Faster he worked her, his fingers slipping in and out of her slippery sex, the friction on her clit coiling her need tighter and tighter. Her orgasm hit, and she buried her face in the curve of his shoulder, sinking her teeth into his flesh as she shook with the intensity of her climax. Slowly, the aching tremors in her flesh subsided, and he withdrew his hand and pulled down her skirt.

Teddy wanted to chastise him. Scurry out in embarrassment. Something. But people always said revenge was the best remedy. She slunk from her chair and positioned herself between his knees.

"Teddy," he growled in soft warning. Too late.

Her hands unsnapped the closure to his pants, and his cock sprang out into her waiting hands. She clasped and stroked him, for the first time truly exploring his rod, a velvet-covered steel shaft. Her thumb brushed the tip of his mushroom head and smoothed the wet drop pearling there. She tilted forward and took him in her mouth.

He bucked, and she let go of his length to brace her palms on his thighs. The taste of him and his reaction—threading his fingers in her hair—made her bolder. She inhaled him, deep then deeper. She clamped her lips tight around him and suctioned as she pulled back. The rigidity of his body told her how much he enjoyed that. Again and again, she bobbed her head down then up, sucking intently.

She increased her pace and knew he'd reached his peak when his grip in her hair tightened almost painfully. He thrust once up into her mouth just as he came, the hotness of his cream filling her mouth. She swallowed and then licked him clean. She pulled his hands free and snuck back into her seat, unable to stop her self-satisfied grin.

Later, she'd allow herself to succumb to embarrassment. Right after she told him that couldn't happen again, enjoyable as it had been.

I've got to get him away before I forget myself and fall in love.

WORDS FAILED Reece as they drove back to her place in silence. What had begun as a tease in the movie theatre had ended up in a loss of control—not that he hadn't enjoyed it. On the contrary, he couldn't wait to repeat it. Over and over.

But dammit, I meant to only arouse her, bring her to the edge and drive her wild. He'd accomplished that and then hadn't stopped. Even more astonishing, she'd reciprocated.

Perhaps her family was wrong. Her actions seemed to indicate she'd accepted him. They pulled up to her house, and she hopped out before he could come around to help her.

She fled to her door, and when he moved to follow her inside, she whirled and blocked him. "Thank you for a nice evening."

He arched his brow. Nice? She called what they'd done nice? "Who says it's done?"

"I do. I'm a teacher and a respected member of this community. I can't go out with you and do things like that. It's indecent."

"I didn't see you arguing."

"Yeah, well, I let my hormones dictate my actions there, but now that my mind is clear again, we can't ever do that again."

Reece wanted to growl at her stubbornness. "Let's go inside and discuss this."

She shook her head. "Nope. I don't trust you not

to try and use your manly wiles on me. And I've got to work in the morning."

His stubborn Teddy bear needed a good shake—followed by a great shag—but he held back. "Fine. Go to bed, alone. I'll see you in the morning when I drive you."

"There's no need. My car's back."

Reece turned to look and saw her car parked in the shadows. The click of the door announced she'd used his inattention to hide.

Reece sighed. He could have busted down her door and pushed the issue, but he didn't. He'd seen the uncertainty in her eyes, the fear her mother had warned him about. He didn't want to goad her into running. *Baby steps*, he reminded himself. He'd accomplished a lot this evening, and whether she liked it or not, she'd go to sleep thinking of him.

And besides, he had things to take care of, starting with her car.

CHAPTER 8

*T*eddy woke the next day in a disgruntled mood. Sure, she'd done the right thing in sending Reece away. She'd had no choice, considering how wonderful the evening turned out.

How am I supposed to fight him off when he keeps doing nice things? Not to mention, the naughty things kept making her blood boil.

She almost expected to see him again when she got out of the shower and tried to tell herself it wasn't disappointment she felt when she had to grab her own towel. Her kitchen was also empty when she came down, and she stifled a sob.

I guess he got the point and left.

Her reaction to his lack of appearance just reinforced her belief she'd done the right thing in sending him away before she fell in love with him.

Swinging between tears and anger over being right about him, she banged out of her house and locked the door, never knew when a hairy varmint might try and sneak in. A varmint she just might shoot!

Only when she turned did her violent ire melt. Her breath caught. Leaning against his truck, unshaven and hotter than ever, stood Reece.

Perverseness made her say, "I told you I was going to drive myself."

"That might be kind of hard without a car."

His answer startled her, and she flicked her gaze around to notice that her car had indeed disappeared. She scowled at him. "What did you do to my car?"

He smiled, a sensuous, lazy grin that touched her in places that warmed and tingled. "It needed a tune-up. So I took it somewhere. Could be a while before it gets back, they tell me. I guess you're stuck with me as a chauffeur again."

Teddy gave up. She couldn't keep fighting him and, even more annoyingly, herself. She shook her head as she walked toward him. *I can handle this. I just need to make sure my heart stays out of it.* "Fine, you can drive me, but don't think I'm going to let your hairy ass sleep in my bed."

He chuckled as he gave her a hug. "Who says we'd

sleep?" He then kissed her, a thorough embrace that made her knees give out.

"Time to get you to class," he said huskily, breaking the kiss. He swung her into the seat of his truck and drove her to work, with her aware of him the entire time.

The day was a repeat of the previous one with her unable to scrub him from her thoughts and anxiously counting the minutes until her day was done.

He picked her up at five minutes after three, but instead of going back to her place, once again, he surprised her and took her out, this time bowling.

It was only as they munched on nachos and sipped Cokes that she cocked her head and asked him, "Who told you I bowled?"

"I've got my sources."

It flattered her to realize he'd made the effort to find out what she liked.

Once again, they talked and enjoyed themselves. While sexual awareness tingled between them, it wasn't the focal point. Laughter and a good time bowling and chatting took precedence. It helped that, in the bright neon lights, there was nowhere for them to get frisky, although they couldn't stop the quick kisses and furtive caresses.

By the time they left and got into his truck, her

whole body tingled. Silence fell between them as the sexual tension mounted. Teddy knew what would happen when they got back to her place. And truthfully, she didn't have the strength or will to stop it. She wanted him. Even knowing—and fearing—it wouldn't last, she couldn't resist his allure any longer.

Just the thought of him touching her made moisture wet her cleft. Her nipples hardened into tight buds. She couldn't stop staring at his hands, clenching the steering wheel. Strong hands that she wanted to feel on her skin.

She took the initiative for the first time and placed her hand on his firm thigh. She heard him blow out noisily.

"Teddy, what are you doing?"

Desire made her mouth dry, and besides, she didn't know what to reply without sounding like a brazen hussy. Instead, showed him what she wanted. She slid her hand over to rub against the ever-present bulge at his groin. The truck swerved and slowed to a stop. Seconds later, he'd dragged her onto his lap and claimed her lips. She clung to him, wiggling her bottom against his groin. She wanted him, and she kept shifting, trying to get closer, but the steering wheel prodded her back, an annoying distraction to the feel of his mouth on hers.

As if sensing her dilemma, he reclined the seat so she could straddle him. When her pants proved difficult to remove in the confines of the truck cab, he ripped the seams. Hot didn't begin to describe that action. Naked from the waist down and wet enough to wring, she sat on his cock, the restricted space of the cab making it a little difficult to find a comfortable position, but they managed. She rode him, her fingers digging into the flesh of his chest where she braced herself. His hands on her waist guided her into a rhythm that had both of them panting and climaxing while the windows of the truck fogged over.

They eventually continued the drive home but never made it to her bed. He fondled her bare bottom as he carried her into the house. Impatient, they made it as far as the couch, where he bent her over and plowed her. When they'd finished, she snuggled up to him with a contented sigh, her eyes drooping. He carried her upstairs and tucked her into bed before sliding in beside her.

Cradled in his arms, Teddy wished she could have him this way forever.

CHAPTER 9

*R*eece was in love. Completely and utterly head over heels. Over the past week, as he'd gotten to know Teddy both in a mental and carnal sense, he'd discovered she was everything he'd ever wanted or needed in a woman. Who knew he needed a funny little spitfire with a heart of gold?

And I do need her and want her so badly. Every moment with her was precious, a voyage of discovery into what made her smile and tick. Then add to all that wondrousness, the awe he couldn't help that she carried his child. *That's my pup in her belly.* A fact she seemed still woefully oblivious of.

Even more astonishing than the revelation of how he truly felt was the fact she'd softened toward him and no longer fought him tooth and nail. She didn't bother to hid her smiles of happiness when she saw him. Even better, she'd started initiating their hugs, among other things. But it wasn't just about sex. They talked. They played. They slept together at night. And yes, they made love everywhere. Well, everywhere except in a bed. Their couplings tended to be spur-of-the-moment and impatient. By the time they made it to bed, exhausted, she tended to snuggle against him and fall asleep.

He kept meaning to make love to her in the morning when they woke in bed, but events kept conspiring against that plan, from the alarm clock not going off to her mom calling to him satisfying her in the shower because he couldn't help himself. It made Reece wonder if they were doomed to only quick, frantic bouts.

He drove her to work every morning, leaving her with a hot kiss that made her eyes glow. He picked her up every day, and while they never managed to make it home before having to pull over, he couldn't complain. He'd rather enjoyed her blushes when he had to wash the ass marks off the hood.

But even amidst the happiness and sex, he could never quite dispel the shadow in her eyes. The way he'd catch her looking at him, her pearly white teeth worrying at her lower lip. Reece knew she still believed he'd leave her, and he'd had enough. He was going to tell her she was pregnant and wake her up to the fact that it wasn't hormones that made him stay, but her.

Today, right after work. With it being Friday, that gave him the whole weekend to prove to her over and over that he loved her and her body. He also had the ring that he intended to present to her once she finally admitted she loved him, too.

That is, once I find her, dammit. He arrived at the school, only to discover Teddy had left early, claiming she felt ill. And she wasn't the only one. A sick feeling also invaded him as he searched for her high and low, but she'd vanished seemingly without a trace.

Reality knocked hard on his bubble of happiness. *Ah, Teddy bear, why did you have to run away?*

&

THE DAY for her period came and went without a sign. Teddy almost sank to the floor in tears. The week that passed had been fantastic. She'd loved every moment, and now because Reece had succeeded in impregnating her, it was all about to end. Even worse, she knew it would destroy her to see him pay the same attention to another.

Maybe I'm wrong. Periods were sometimes late. It didn't mean she was knocked up.

Teddy attempted to act normal that morning when he drove her to work. She knew he sensed something wrong by the cease at his brow, but she smiled brightly and kissed him as if nothing was amiss. But as soon as he'd driven out of sight, she went into action. She excused herself at the office, saying she didn't feel well, and went to the pharmacy. She braved the knowing smiles of the cashier—a second cousin—and hurried to the coffee shop and its public washroom.

The confirmation on the little plastic stick made her heart sink. Tears rolled down her cheeks. The mating fever had done its job. She was pregnant, and without the mating hormones driving him, Reece would lose his blinders and see her once again for who she was. A short and chubby woman, not his type at all. Her heart cracked.

Teddy called and asked a cousin of hers to give her a lift home, claiming a headache. Once there, she couldn't help noting the traces of Reece all over, taunting her. She cried some more as the harshness of the situation kept hammering its point home. *I can't stay.*

Cowardly, but Teddy knew she couldn't handle seeing disinterest in his eyes. She needed to run and hide, wait for him to come to his senses and leave. Run from the heartache she couldn't handle. And she knew the perfect place to make her escape. She didn't pack a bag because she didn't intend to take her car.

She stripped and stowed her clothes in her closet before heading outside naked. She slipped into her bearskin, ignoring her beast's chuffing question, and waddled into the woods. She already knew Reece was a damned good tracker. So she had to be smart, although now that the crazy urge to mate was gone, there was a good chance he wouldn't even bother looking.

She splashed into the stream that ran for miles and branched off in numerous places. She stayed in its chilly flow, working her way up its meandering path, hiding her tracks.

The route she took ended up longer, but after hours of backtracking to hide any trace of her passage, she finally arrived at the cabin her family owned, high up in the chilly, mountainous peaks. She switched back to her human form and shivered, more from the gravity of what she'd done than cold. She opened the door to the rustic cabin and slipped in.

His scent, so unexpected in this secret place, sent her running right back outside. Not far, of course. She'd barely gone five feet when he tackled her naked body with his. The ground approached fast, but she never met its hard surface because he made sure to grab her and roll so that he hit the ground before she did.

His strong arms wrapped tightly around her, and plastered to his chest, she could only look into his face. Sparking eyes met hers, and at his stormy expression, she bit her lip.

"I can explain."

"No, you can't. I thought we'd gotten past this tendency of yours to run away from me."

Shame made her drop her eyes and stare at his mouth.

"What's it going to take for you to understand I want you and have no intention of ever leaving?" His tight voice, so angry and disappointed, hit her hard.

Tears pricked her eyes, and she couldn't answer. With the proof of her pregnancy, she knew it was only a matter of time before he broke that promise.

How he managed to get up off the ground without letting go of her, she couldn't figure out. He carried her into the cabin, and Teddy didn't bother fighting. She wouldn't win.

"What are you going to do?" she whispered when he dropped her on the large bed covered in faded quilts. Naked as they both were, she couldn't help the warmth that shot through her, especially when she realized that, for once, they'd made it to a bed before giving in to their desire.

"You just never learn," said Reece, his exasperation clear. He stood at the foot of the bed and stared down at her. "So, I'm going to make love to you, slowly."

Teddy's brow creased. That didn't sound so bad, so why did he look so apologetic? He clambered onto the bed and straddled her. Teddy gasped at the strangely intimate position. He leaned over her, and his lips brushed hers. His hands caught hers and stretched them over her head. Too distracted by the way his lips slid over hers in a slow tease, she didn't immediately react when his hand around her wrist was replaced by something cold, but when it happened to her second wrist, her eyes shot open. She pulled at her arms, but they were caught. She craned her head and saw leather cuffs manacling her to the headboard.

"What are you doing?" she screeched.

"You have this annoying tendency of running away whenever I think I've made progress. So, I'm going to keep you here until you finally admit you love me and promise you won't ever leave again."

"Never. Let me go this instant."

"Nope," he calmly replied, tying down her thrashing legs.

"You'll never get away with this. My mother will hunt you down and eat you," she threatened.

"Who do you think told me how to get here before you?" he replied, growling against her ear.

Treacherous family. Teddy pulled at the restraints, but they didn't budge, and she screamed. "I hate you. Why won't you just leave?"

"Because I love you!" he shouted back. "When are you going to get it through your thick bear skull that I want to be with you, forever?"

Tears pricked her eyes. "No, you don't. It won't be long now. You'll suddenly see me again the way you did that first time. Please let me go before that happens and you hurt me."

His large hands cupped her face, and the eyes that looked into hers were moist. If she didn't know better, she'd swear he looked in pain. "Aw, Teddy bear. Don't cry."

She didn't reply and turned her head, letting her tears soak the pillow he placed under her head.

"Go on, do your worst," she dared him through a throat clogged with tears. "Spank me. Hit me. Nothing you do to my body can rival the pain in my heart."

"Why the hell would I hurt you? Anyone ever tell you that you're a drama queen?"

His goading comment made her face him with a glare. "And you're a pain in the ass, wolf."

"Hmm, not yet, but if you're into that, we can arrange it."

Teddy blushed and stammered. "N-no, I'm not. Would you stop joking? This isn't funny."

"Yes, it is," he replied solemnly, only to grin at her a moment later. "I love you, Teddy bear, even if you drive me mental. I love you. You and the babe you carry."

She froze. "You know?"

"I've known for a while. I hate to break it to you, Teddy, but I knocked you up that first night."

"No way. I don't believe you."

Reece sighed. "You are so stubborn sometimes. Listen carefully. I have known since the dinner at your mother's. It's not mating hormones keeping me around. Haven't you noticed that our reaction to each other changed since that first night we met?"

She frowned and opened her mouth to refute. Then stopped. *What's he talking about? We've been doing it like bunnies every time we see each other.* However, not since that first time had her bear roused and tried to take control and force the issue. Not since that first time had she felt that strange, almost out-of-body sensation. "I don't understand."

"For a smart bear, sometimes you're as dense as a woodchuck. I'm attracted to you, mating instinct or not. The first time we made love, I didn't just impregnate you. I discovered that my previous aversion to girls with curves was stupid. Actually, more than stupid. Do you know how much more fun it is to plow into your sweet, soft flesh? To bury my face between your plush tits and smother myself? To take you from behind and slap up against your awesome ass?"

"But—but—"

"But what?"

"That would mean you like me, curves and all."

"Love you," he corrected. "Just like I told you I would. We're mates, Teddy, and not just because of hormones or some weird shape-shifter godly force. I love you because you're smart and sweet. I love you because you like corny alien flicks. I love the fact you blush. I love that you can't cook a steak if your life depended on it. I love that you don't mind wearing white around children and, even better, smile when they get you dirty. I love that you're soft enough to handle my big, hard body. I love that you're short and I can pick you up and make love to you anywhere I like. I love that you're wild and leave scratches in my back because I've pleasured you so well. How many other ways would you like me to show you I love you?"

Her heart swelled at his declaration, but fear just wouldn't let her go. "But what about when I get big with the babe growing in me?"

He placed his hand over her stomach. "I will love

you even more as the mother of our child. I will worship every pound you gain as a sign of your love for me and our babe."

"Prove it." The husky words slipped from her, and she shivered when his eyes darkened with desire.

CHAPTER 10

Those two words, "prove it", along with the hopeful look in her eyes, packed a punch. He almost asked her if she wanted him to fetch her the moon because, in that moment, he'd have given her anything. He decided to show her how much he cared in the only way he knew how, by worshipping the body she feared he'd reject. What a fabulous chore.

While he'd had many opportunities over the last week to enjoy her body, and catch glimpses, this was his first unrushed view. And he meant to make the most of it. Once he was done worshipping at the altar of her curves, there'd be no room in her mind for doubt that he loved every inch of her.

She lay there, her eyes hooded with desire, but he could see the tremble of fear. He made sure she saw him look her over and the evidence of his enjoyment—his cock throbbing and hard.

He ran a finger down her body, from the hollow at the base of her throat, through the valley between her breasts, over the rounded softness of her belly to the curls at the vee of her thighs.

"Beautiful," he murmured. So much of her enticed him that he found himself at a loss as to where to start. He commenced at the top.

He kissed the pulse that fluttered at her throat and, from there, slid his mouth across skin softer than any silk to the generous mound of her breast. He didn't immediately latch onto her nipple, although it did beckon. He twirled, instead, his tongue around that puckered aureole. He rubbed the edge of his bristled jaw against her tender skin, forcing her to gasp and sigh.

When he opened his mouth wide over her bud and finally tasted it, she cried out. He forced himself to take it slowly, sucking and teasing the protruding berry before switching to perform the same torture on the other.

"Please."

He heard her plea and ignored it. He'd spent all week taking her like a savage. It was time he found some self-control and pleasured her the way she deserved. The aroma of her desire wafted up to tickle his nose, and he had to bury his face between her breasts and grit his teeth against the temptation to sink into her glorious warmth.

He breathed deep, his warm breath moistening her skin. When he felt ready to continue, he kissed his way down her torso, stopping at her navel to tickle her with his tongue.

"Reece!" She bucked under him, and he nipped her skin.

"I'm done letting you distract me from exploring and tasting you," he growled in reply. He heard her swallow as he continued his descent, pausing to nuzzle his face in her pubes. She quivered, and her breathing hitched. He drew out her agony, kissing the inside of her tender thigh. Blowing gently on her sex. He even gave her one quick lick that made her arch. But he denied himself his prize to kiss the other thigh.

"Re-e-e-ece," she moaned, and he shuddered.

He wanted to plunge his cock into her so badly, but he denied himself in favor of tasting her climax on his tongue first.

He placed his mouth on her molten core and slid his tongue between her plump lips. Her channel quivered wetly about his tongue, and her exquisite flavor just about made him come.

She keened loudly and thrashed, her body jerking as he explored her with his lips and tongue. He placed one hand on her lower stomach to hold her down and lost himself in the pleasure of her pussy. She responded like a wanton woman at his touch, and he reveled in it. He flicked his tongue against her clit and inserted two fingers into her sex. Her channel clamped down tightly on his digits, and a few strokes of his tongue over her nub was all it took for her to come screaming. The pulsing feel of her on his fingers was too much for him. He positioned himself over her, the tip of his cock rubbing against her.

She looked so beautiful lying there, her face flushed with passion, and her eyes, when they opened, glowed.

"Tell me," he demanded. "Please, Teddy bear," he pled, needing to hear the words.

§⁂

TEDDY HEARD his request through the blood pumping fiercely through her body. Heard his plea and saw it in his eyes, eyes that looked at her without flinching, even though the mating hormone was no more.

He sees me, and he loves me. There was no disgust or disappointment in his eyes. On the contrary, his gaze held a fierce possessiveness. He'd seen her, all of her, without the rose-colored vision of a man in the grips of the mating lust, and even though she wasn't model perfect, he wanted her.

She couldn't deny it to him or herself any longer. "I love you." The words made his face light up, and he'd never looked more gorgeous to her than at that moment. "I love you," she said again, laughing even as she cried.

He swooped down and kissed her as he thrust into her. Her hips arched up to greet his pumping body. Together, they moved in rhythm, their bodies intimately joined, but nothing compared to the closeness of their hearts that beat in time.

In the moment before her orgasm, she opened her eyes and found him already watching her. Her climax hit, and she screamed his name. She tried to show him with her eyes what she felt in her heart. Love, a love reciprocated in his bellowing cry and in the brightness of his gaze locked with hers.

Only once their pleasure cooled down did he release her from the restraints. He gathered her in his arms with a tenderness that made her eyes prickle again.

"Is it me, or is the pregnancy making you emotional?" he asked, stroking his hands over her.

"Shut up," she muttered, sniffling.

"Hey, I didn't say it was a bad thing. Actually, I think it's kind of cute. Which reminds me, I've got a present for you." Reece rolled out of bed, only to return a moment later with a box that was wet with wolf slobber and covered in teeth marks.

Teddy held her breath as he opened the box and revealed the ring, the ring she'd always dreamed of owning if she ever found the one.

"I love you, Teddy bear. Will you do me the honor of not just being my mate, but my wife as well?"

Crying and laughing at the same time, she nodded her head furiously and threw her arms around his neck, clutching him tightly. "Yes," she choked out, overwhelmed.

LATER THAT NIGHT, Reece held the woman he loved close, thankful he'd found her safe and, even better, finally made her believe. He knew that, while he'd overcome the first major battle—getting her to admit her feelings—he'd have to be sure to show her every day how much he cared. A lifetime of hurt and fear wouldn't be banished in one day, but the road to her full trust was something he would do, no matter how long it took.

Because you're mine, and I couldn't be happier with my chubby Teddy bear.

EPILOGUE

Teddy rubbed her belly as she waited for the ring signaling the end of the school day. With her due date so close, this was her last day of teaching, and her aching lower back thanked her for that fact.

She peered out the window and saw Reece pull into the parking lot with his truck. He hopped out, and her heart fluttered. It didn't matter how many times she saw him, she could never help the smile and happiness that his simple presence caused. He'd shown her in so many ways how much he loved her that, at times, it awed her.

He'd given up everything to be with her—his home, his family and his pack, saying, "You need your family. I just need you." Needless to say, those words got him mauled in a way that left them both flushed and sticky.

Even though he'd chosen to join her pack, she made a point of ensuring they visited his grandmother often. Teddy quite enjoyed the woman who'd raised Reece, especially the stories she regaled her with about his naughty escapades in his youth.

Every day, actually, she found more and more reasons to love her big, bad wolf. True to his word and his love, the bigger she'd grown, the more he'd showered her with attention and affection. Instead of shriveling his desire, her increased girth made him even more amorous. He had a tendency after making tender love to her to rub her belly and grin. The first time he'd done it, she'd asked him why he looked so pleased. He'd cupped her distended abdomen and said, "I helped make this."

Weird, but she loved him anyway.

Still in her position at the window, she scowled as she saw the mothers swarm him. Her bear growled in her head, not happy that these females thought to poach on her territory, but she and her sow were appeased when he didn't pay them so much as a second glance. He strode right up to the school and, a moment later, appeared in her classroom with a broad grin.

"Ready, Teddy bear?"

She stuck her tongue out at him and giggled at his pained look. "Don't do that to me," he admonished. "You know the doc said no more outdoor lovemaking, or on the hood, or…"

Teddy laughed harder. Her poor wolf, forced to make love to her only in a soft bed. She stopped laughing a moment later when a gush of liquid from between her legs soaked her feet.

"Um, Reece, I think the babe is coming."

His expression of sheer panic set her off laughing again, which, in turn, caused her to gush more warm liquid. To his credit, he didn't cringe when he swung her up in his arms and she leaked all over him.

And although he blanched—and swayed—in the birthing room as she screamed during the birth of their very big boy, he managed to stay upright—barely.

"Oh, Teddy," he breathed when he held their son, pride shining moistly in eyes, "he's beautiful."

Teddy agreed, although, in her case, it had more to with the expression on her husband's face. In that moment, the final brick in the way of her trust crumbled to dust. Together, she and Reece had formed a family pack of their own, one that would only grow. She knew to the depths of her being that no other woman, no fate, no force at all, would ever tear Reece from her side because she was his chubby

Teddy bear, and he loved her more than life itself, which happened to be exactly how she loved him. A true love that would last forever, thick or thin.

The End

www.ingramcontent.com/pod-product-compliance
Lightning Source LLC
LaVergne TN
LVHW041645060526
838200LV00040B/1714